Headless Halloween

Look for more books in the Goosebumps Series 2000
by R.L. Stine:

Headless Halloween

AN
APPLE
PAPERBACK

SCHOLASTIC INC.
New York Toronto London Auckland Sydney

A PARACHUTE PRESS BOOK

ISBN 0-590-76781-X

Copyright © 1998 by Parachute Press, Inc.
All rights reserved. Published by Scholastic Inc.
APPLE PAPERBACKS and logo are trademarks and/or registered trademarks of Scholastic Inc.
GOOSEBUMPS is a registered trademark of Parachute Press, Inc.

12 11 10 9 8 7 6 5 4 3 2 1   8 9/9 0 1 2 3/0

Printed in the U.S.A.   40

First Scholastic printing, October 1998

1

"YAAAAIIIIII!"

That's the sound of terror. A loud, bloodcurdling scream.

I love it.

I know, I know. It's kind of sick. But I can't help it.

My name is Brandon Plush. And my motto is "Make 'Em Scream."

I love scaring people. I love hearing kids gasp in surprise — and then shriek their heads off.

It's so funny. True panic — it always makes me laugh.

Dad says I have a cruel streak. He says I get it from him. The two of us stay up late watching horror movies on TV. We always laugh when people get sliced and diced or eaten by monsters.

1

Mom says I have to be nicer to people. Whenever she says that, Dad and I share a secret smile. We know that *scary* is *fun*.

My sister, Maya, is seven, and she is the perfect victim. Maya screams if you cross your eyes at her. She's scared of bugs, worms, dogs, cats, bats, and even some kinds of birds.

She's a great kid, and she's terrified of me. I can make her scream with one hand tied behind my back.

Last night, I hid in her closet wearing one of the ugliest masks from my scary mask collection.

The man who sold it to me told me it was a one-of-a-kind mask.

"Nobody else has anything like it," he said.

When Maya opened the closet door, I growled like a wild animal and came leaping out at her in my mask.

The poor kid screamed, and spit up her entire dinner.

Ha ha. Did I laugh? I couldn't stop!

I told you, she's the perfect victim.

"Brandon — why did you do that?" Mom demanded. She wasn't happy. She had to clean up the mess.

"Oops!" I replied. "Just joking."

That's my other motto: "Oops — just joking."

Did I scare ten years off your life? Did I scare you out of your skin? *Oops — just joking!*

My cousin Vinnie lives down the block. He's nearly as bad as Maya. Vinnie is eleven, just a year younger than me. But he's a scrawny little nerd.

If he was big enough to have a shadow, he'd be terrified of it!

I can scare Vinnie in my sleep.

On Saturday, I found a fat purple worm in the backyard. When Vinnie came over, I slipped the worm down the back of his sweater. I told him it was a poisonous snake.

Did he *scream*?

Ha ha! He set a world record.

Then Vinnie froze as the worm slid down his back. His eyes practically popped out of his head, and his teeth began to chatter.

Finally, I reached down his back, pulled out the worm, and held it up to Vinnie's face. "Oops — just joking!" I told him.

Then I laughed for a week.

Vinnie just stood there shaking. He cracks me up. He really does.

Vinnie and Maya and a lot of other kids in my neighborhood are in major trouble. That's because it's nearly Halloween — my favorite time of the year.

I have *big* plans for Halloween.

I plan to go headless this year.

Jennifer and Ray are two little kids who live across the street from Vinnie. Sometimes when their parents can't find anyone else, they ask me to baby-sit.

Guess why I love to baby-sit for the two brats.

That's right.

They're total 'fraidy cats.

I can make them scream with my eyes shut.

I love to tell them scary stories. I tell them stories that make their flesh creep. That curdle their blood. That make their hair stand on end.

They always scream till they choke. And if my story is *really* good, sometimes I can make them cry.

Ha ha!

They're pitiful. You've got to love it!

A few nights ago, I was down the block baby-sitting for them. I led the two little angels down to the rec room in the basement.

"I'm going to tell you a true story," I said.

"Please don't tell a scary story!" Jennifer begged.

"Please don't scare us tonight," Ray whined.

You should have seen how sweet they looked, begging me to go easy on them.

But I turned the lights real low, and I told them the scariest ghost story I could think of. I used my creepy, whispery voice. And I spoke real softly, so they had to lean in close to hear.

"Your parents don't want you to know this," I started. "But it's a true story."

Their eyes grew wider. I could see they were scared already!

"Another family used to live in your house," I told them. "They had a boy and a girl about your age. But the boy and the girl didn't last long. Something *horrible* happened to them. Right in this basement. Right in this room."

"Please stop," Ray begged.

Jennifer had her hands over her ears. But I knew she could still hear me.

"I don't like this story," Ray whined.

"I don't like it, either," his sister agreed.

"It gets better," I told them.

I took a deep breath and started again in a whisper. "Did you know your house is haunted?" I asked.

Their mouths dropped open.

"Well, the boy and girl didn't know. They didn't know that a very cruel ghost lived down in this basement. The ghost stayed quiet most of the time. But it had one bad habit."

"Please stop," Jennifer begged in a trembling voice.

"Yeah. Let's go upstairs," Ray pleaded.

"Every year, just before Halloween, the ghost liked to murder anyone who came down to this room," I continued. "'The basement is mine,' the ghost declared. 'If someone comes down here, I'll make them suffer. I'll turn them into ghosts too.'"

"This isn't true — is it?" Jennifer asked in a tiny voice.

"It's just a story — right?" her wimpy little brother added.

"Of course it's true," I answered. "It happened right over there." I pointed.

"*What* happened?" Jennifer asked.

"The boy and girl didn't know about the ghost. They came down to the basement to play. They were down on the floor, right over there." I pointed again.

"Slowly . . . slowly . . . the ghost crept up behind the boy. Closer . . . Closer . . ."

"Please!" Jennifer begged, covering her ears again.

"Please — stop!" Copycat Ray covered his ears too.

"Closer . . . ," I whispered. "The ghost floated closer. It stretched out its cold, dead arms . . . curled and uncurled its bony, dead fingers. It reached out . . . reached out — AND PULLED OFF THE BOY'S HEAD!" I screamed, grabbing Ray by the throat.

Both kids let out horrified shrieks.

"Wh-what happened to the girl?" Jennifer stuttered.

"She ran away," I told them. "She was never seen again. That's why their parents sold this house to your parents."

"But the boy —?" Ray started.

"The headless boy is still down here," I whispered. I looked around, as if searching for him. "The headless boy haunts the basement now. Waiting. Waiting for fresh victims."

"That's a lie!" Jennifer cried, jumping to her feet. "It's just a story — right? There is no headless boy down here."

"Brandon, can we *please* go upstairs?" Ray begged. He grabbed his sister's hand and held on to it for dear life.

They were both so scared, they were shaking like Jell-O.

Maybe I should have given them a break. Maybe I should have stopped there.

But I had a brilliant idea.

7

"Sit down," I ordered them. "Don't move. I'm going to prove that the headless boy lives here. I'll be right back."

They begged me not to leave them there. But I ran upstairs and found my bag. I always bring a bag of special stuff with me on baby-sitting jobs. You know. Masks and props to help me scare the kiddies to death.

I pulled out the ugly rubber mask I'd brought. It had stringy blue hair, gobs of green rubber slime pouring from empty eye sockets, and deep cuts and scabs all over its face.

"Perfect," I murmured to myself. I guess I was grinning from ear to ear. My plan was so *awesome*!

I quickly made myself headless. It was easy. I pulled my shirt up and buttoned it over my head. My head was completely hidden.

Then I bent a coat hanger and made it stand up from my shirt collar. And I slid the ugly mask over the hanger, onto my shoulders.

I checked myself in the front hall mirror. Yes! The mask now looked like my head.

Show time!

I made my way down the stairs and staggered into the rec room. "I'm the headless boy!" I cried in a deep, scary voice. "I'm the headless one who haunts the basement."

Ray screamed. But Jennifer just sneered at me. "We know it's you, Brandon," she said.

"I'm the headless one," I repeated. "Go ahead. Pull off the mask."

They hesitated.

"Pull off the mask," I repeated.

Finally, Jennifer stepped forward. She raised both hands to the sides of the mask and tugged it off.

No head!

No head underneath!

They screamed so hard, the walls shook. And then they started to cry.

Both of them. Wailing in terror.

A great moment.

But it lasted only a moment.

Because I turned toward the stairs — and it was *my* turn to scream!

I screamed because both parents stood at the bottom of the steps.

They didn't look too happy.

I poked my head up from under the shirt.

"What's wrong?" the mom asked. She went running to the crying kids. "Kids? What's wrong? What happened?"

The dad glared at me angrily. "Why are they crying, Brandon?"

I shrugged. "Beats me," I replied. "Maybe something scared them."

When I got home, I called my best friend, Cal. Cal is big. He's nearly six feet tall, and he weighs at least a ton. Maybe two tons.

He can be pretty scary when he wants to be.

And he likes to pick on kids who *aren't* his size — which is why he's my best friend.

"Cal, I just did the coolest thing," I told him. "I terrified these two kids by making myself headless."

"Cool," Cal replied. But I could tell he didn't know what I was talking about.

It took me a while to explain the whole thing to him. Then he said "Cool" again.

"Let's go headless on Halloween," I suggested. "If we both go headless, we can *really* make kids scream."

"Excellent," Cal replied. "And maybe we can lock some kids in the haunted house. You know. The old house at the dead end."

Cal and I had a lot of fun locking kids in the haunted house. Then we'd wait outside and listen to them scream.

"I can't wait," Cal said.

I had to hang up the phone. Mom was calling me from downstairs.

"Don't have a cow! I'm coming!" I shouted.

I could tell she was angry. Mom has long red hair, and she flings it from side to side when she's angry. Both of her hands were balled into tight fists.

"Brandon, Mrs. Sullivan just phoned me," Mom said through gritted teeth.

"Uh-oh." I gulped. Mrs. Sullivan is Jennifer and Ray's mom.

"She forgot to pay me," I said. "Is that why she called?"

Mom swung her hair from side to side. "That's not why she called," she snapped.

"Uh-oh." I gulped again.

"Mrs. Sullivan said you terrified her kids," Mom continued. "She can't get them to stop crying. She said she'll never use you as a baby-sitter again."

"Never?"

"Never."

I lowered my head. "Sorry," I murmured.

That usually works.

Whenever I'm in major trouble, I lower my head and mutter "Sorry" as softly and sincerely as I can. And that's usually the end of it.

It didn't seem to be working this time.

"Sorry." I muttered it again.

"You're sorry?" Mom cried. "But why do you do it, Brandon? Why are you always scaring kids?"

"Because it's fun?" I replied.

In school the next morning, I was carrying a glass beaker to the science lab. I stopped in the hall to watch Cal stuff a fourth grader into a locker.

The kid asked for it. He stepped on Cal's new Air Jordans. It was an accident. But Cal had no choice. He jammed the poor kid into the locker, slammed the door, and locked it.

I flashed the big guy a thumbs-up. Then I continued on my way, holding the beaker in both hands.

I turned the corner — and saw cousin Vinnie heading my way.

The little wimp had his head buried in a book. He was reading as he walked down the hall, and he didn't see me.

"Vinnie — look out!" I called. "I'm carrying this acid to the science lab."

He glanced up — just as I tripped.

The liquid flew up from the beaker —

— and splashed over Vinnie.

Over his head, his face, and down the front of his shirt.

And we both opened our mouths in screams of horror.

"**M**y face! My eyes!" Vinnie wailed. He dropped to his knees and folded his body into a quivering ball.

"Oh, be quiet. It's only water," I told him.

"Huh?" The little geek opened his eyes. "Only water?"

"Oops — just joking!" I cried.

He swallowed a couple of times. Then he brushed water from his face with both hands. "That wasn't funny, Brandon," he muttered angrily.

"Yes, it was," I replied.

"*No, it wasn't funny!*" boomed a deep voice from close behind me.

I spun around, nearly dropping the empty glass beaker. "Mr. Benson?" I gasped.

My least favorite teacher.

14

He clapped a big hand on my shoulder. "Not funny, Brandon," he repeated. He had a voice like a bass drum. Even when he whispered, the words came out loud.

Mr. Benson is about ten feet tall and all muscle. Behind his back, kids call him "Mountain."

He has thick black hair that he pulls back into a ponytail. And bushy black eyebrows that dance up and down on his forehead like two caterpillars.

He wears faded jeans and big, flannel shirts. And he has a tiny silver ring in one ear.

A lot of kids think he's cool. But I don't like him much. He's very strict in his science classes. And he always seems to have his eye on me.

Like now.

"Brandon, I saw the whole thing," Mr. Benson boomed. "I saw your little joke from beginning to end."

"Oh," I replied. What else could I say?

"Have you ever heard of the Golden Rule?" he asked, his caterpillar eyebrows going wild. "Do unto others as you would have them do unto you."

"I never heard of that one," I muttered.

A group of kids had gathered around us in the hall. I started to feel embarrassed. Mountain still had his huge paw on my shoulder.

Some girls were asking Vinnie how he got all wet.

Mr. Benson leaned over me. I could smell coffee on his breath. Yuck.

15

"Would you like Vinnie to splash water all over *you*?" he asked.

"I tripped!" I lied. "It was an accident."

Mr. Benson's eyebrows jumped up and down on his broad forehead. He shook his head. "Brandon, I told you, I saw the whole thing," he repeated.

"He told me it was *acid*!" Vinnie chimed in. The little wimp.

A few kids gasped.

"Come with me," Mr. Benson ordered. He began to guide me down the hall.

"But I'll be late for class!" I protested.

"Too bad," Mr. Benson replied. "You and I need to talk. I'm going to give you Lecture Number Three-forty-five."

"What lecture is that?" I grumbled.

"It's all about cruelty to others."

He led me into his science classroom and shut the door. Then he made me sit across from his desk.

He sat on the edge of his desk, hovering over me like a buzzard about to eat its prey.

"For the rest of this week, I'd like you to stay after school and clean the science lab," he said.

"But I didn't mess it up!" I protested.

He ignored that and began his lecture about this Golden Rule thing — about how we have to be nice to other people if we want them to be nice to us.

The lecture seemed to go on for hours. But I

tuned out after the first minute or two. His voice droned on in the background.

I was already planning my revenge.

Mr. Benson, I thought, it's almost Halloween.

You shouldn't get on my case just before Halloween. Because now I have no choice.

Now I have to think up a nice Halloween surprise for *you*!

I stayed after school and cleaned the science lab. It put me in a really bad mood.

The last class had been doing some really smelly experiments. And now I smelled just like the experiments.

I kicked my backpack most of the way home. It was so late, the sun was already starting to go down. Fat brown leaves swirled around my legs in a gusty, fall wind.

Starting up my driveway, I had a really good idea.

I dumped my backpack on the front steps. Then I made my way to the side of the house. I climbed the wide oak tree that nearly touches the house. And I edged out on a limb right outside my sister's bedroom window.

I slid open the window. And I waited.

The lights were on in Maya's room. And her computer screen glowed. I knew she'd come upstairs soon. And when she entered her room, she wouldn't be expecting any visitors. Especially not from the window.

I leaned close to the house and listened. Yes! Footsteps in the hall.

I edged along the tree branch, closer to the window. Then I leaned back so Maya wouldn't see me when she walked into the room.

I held my breath and waited.

Maya stepped into the bedroom. I peeked in. What was she carrying? A bowl of something. And a glass of chocolate milk.

Perfect.

She took a few steps toward her desk.

I leaned forward . . . closer . . .

"AAAAAAAGH!" I opened my mouth in a terrifying shriek — and dove through the window.

Maya's eyes bulged. Her mouth dropped open, but no sound came out. Her hands shot up. And the bowl and glass went flying.

The bowl shattered on the floor. Potato chips flew everywhere. The glass landed on its side, spilling chocolate milk over the white shag rug.

"BRANDON!" Maya shrieked. "You jerk! You JERK!"

"Oops — just joking!" I exclaimed. I started to laugh. I thought I might keep on laughing for at least a year.

Maya started furiously pounding my chest with her fists. But of course, that only made me laugh harder.

"Okay, okay. I'll help you clean up," I told her. I knew I had to calm her down.

I was totally cheered up. It doesn't take much to put me in a good mood. Just a good scare.

"Promise you'll never do that again," Maya insisted.

"Promise," I replied.

"Do you *really* promise?" she demanded. "Really, really?"

"Sure," I said, patting her head. "I *really* promise."

It's easy to make promises. I mean, what *are* promises? Things that are easy to break — right?

I helped her clean up the broken china and the potato chips and chocolate milk. The rug had a big stain in it — but what could I do?

When we finished, Maya started getting her Halloween costume together. What did she plan to be? A princess, of course.

"Brandon, what are you going to be?" she asked, fiddling with the elastic band on a sparkly tiara.

"For trick or treat?" I replied. "I'm not wearing a costume. That's for babies. I'll just scare some kid and grab his bag of candy."

She narrowed her eyes at me. "You're kidding — right?"

I grinned in reply.

20

Why would I kid about a thing like that?

I lowered my voice. "Know what Cal and I are going to do?"

"Something horrible, I'd guess," Maya said, making a face.

"Yeah," I agreed. "Cal and I are going to trash Mr. Benson's house."

"You are not!" Maya declared. She picked up a pink crepe skirt and held it against her waist. "That's stupid."

"Why is it stupid?" I demanded.

"Because *you're* stupid!" she replied nastily.

"You're too stupid to be stupid!" I told her. If she wanted to fight, I was ready.

Maya dropped the skirt to the bed. "That house is too creepy," she said.

She was right about that. Mr. Benson lives in this big, old wreck, very dark and totally falling apart. The house is on the edge of Raven's Ravine.

"You know Mom and Dad said you're not allowed to go near the ravine," Maya sneered.

I repeated those words, mimicking her whiny voice.

She stuck her tongue out at me.

"Bet I could jump the ravine," I bragged.

She gasped. "You're not going to try it — *are* you?"

I grinned. "Maybe."

Actually, I had no plans to try to jump Raven's Ravine.

It was a steep drop, right behind Mr. Benson's house. A rock cliff, like a deep crack in the earth — about ten feet across to the other side.

It's really dangerous. But lots of kids have jumped the ravine on dares.

If you miss, you fall straight down onto the jagged rocks below.

"Don't look for trouble," Maya warned.

"Thanks, *Mom*!" I snapped. "Don't tell me what to do — okay?"

She frowned at me. "If you go to Mr. Benson's house, you'll get caught, Brandon."

"No way," I protested. "Cal and I — we're too fast and too cool."

If only I had listened to her . . .

al called me after dinner on Halloween night. "We're going headless, right?"

"Right," I replied.

"So I don't need a costume, right?"

"Right. You can use one of my masks to put on your shoulders."

"We're not going to trick-or-treat. We're just going to scare kids, right?"

"Right," I repeated. "And we're going to trash Mr. Benson's house."

"Cool," Cal said.

"So hurry over, okay? It's already dark out. Time to get moving."

I grabbed two ugly rubber monster masks from my collection, and hurried downstairs.

A horrible surprise awaited me in the front hall.

A kid in a shiny black Darth Vader costume stepped through the doorway. At first, I thought it was just a trick-or-treater.

But then, through his heavy plastic mask, he said, "Hey, Brandon." And I knew it was Vinnie.

"What are *you* doing here?" I demanded.

Mom walked into the front hall. "Doesn't Vinnie look scary?" she asked. She patted him on top of his plastic head.

"What is he doing here?" I repeated.

"You're taking him trick-or-treating," Mom replied.

I let out a groan.

"And you're taking Maya and her three friends too," Mom announced.

"Excuse me?" I cried. "I'm *what*?"

"You're being a good big brother," Mom replied.

"No way!" I protested. "No way!"

Maya and her three friends came bouncing into the hall. One of them was Ariel the Mermaid. Maya and the other two were all princesses. Yuck.

Maya was pulling on her cardboard tiara. The other two princesses were pushing down their crepe skirts and adjusting their glittery masks. The mermaid was tugging at her fin.

"Let's go," Maya said.

"NO WAY!" I screamed.

Mom narrowed her eyes at me. "I expect you to be a good sport about this, Brandon."

Before I could reply, Cal stuck his head in the front door. "What's up?" he asked.

"You and Brandon are doing a good deed," Mom answered. "You're taking these kids trick-or-treating."

Cal nearly swallowed his tongue. "We are?" he cried.

"Let's go!" Vinnie whined. "It's *hot* inside this mask. I'm sweating!"

Mom stood over me, arms crossed, staring me down. I could see that I had no choice. "No problem," I whispered to Cal. "We'll dump them as fast as we can."

"Okay, okay. Let's go, you guys," I declared. I led the way out the front door.

"Take good care of them," Mom called after me. "And don't let Vinnie get scared."

"Yeah. Sure," I muttered.

I led them across the front lawn toward the neighbors' house. It was a clear, cool night. Wispy clouds wriggled across the full moon like snakes.

The perfect night for scaring kids. But I was stuck with these babies.

The girls were giggling excitedly and talking nonstop. Vinnie held his heavy mask in place with both hands and trotted to keep up.

I could see small groups of trick-or-treaters all the way down the block. Cal and I guided Vinnie and the girls to three or four houses and watched from the driveway as they received their candy.

25

"This isn't any fun," Cal grumbled.

"Let's ditch the geeks," I whispered.

His eyes grew wide. "Huh? Just leave them?"

"Sure. Why not?" I replied.

"But they're only seven!" Cal protested.

"They'll be fine," I told him. "What could happen? They won't even notice we're gone."

Maya and her friends stood in front of an empty lot, talking to another group of girls. I didn't see Vinnie.

"Come on — *run*!" I ordered Cal.

The two of us took off across the street. The girls didn't even see us. We turned the corner and kept running.

After about half a block, I heard footsteps behind us. And Vinnie's whiny voice: "Hey, wait up! Wait up!"

He came running up to us, breathing hard under the mask. Breathing like the real Darth Vader.

"I couldn't see you!" he cried. "It's hard to see in this mask." He started scratching his shoulders, then struggled to scratch his back. "This costume is so itchy. And it's *boiling* in here!"

"Maybe you should have been Princess Leia," I joked.

Vinnie turned his black plastic head from side to side. "Where are the girls?" he asked.

"Uh . . . they decided to go on ahead," I told him.

Cal nodded in agreement. "Maybe you want to catch up to them," he suggested to Vinnie.

"No. I'll stick with you guys," Vinnie replied. "It's kind of scary out here. It's so dark."

Cal and I both sighed. We started walking again. Crossed a street. Then another. Vinnie kept running up to the houses, ringing the doorbells, holding up his Darth Vader trick-or-treat bag for candy.

"He's going to ruin everything," Cal grumbled. "We haven't been able to scare one kid."

"We'll dump him too," I replied. "I have a plan."

"But he's such a wimp," Cal said, shaking his head. "When he sees we're gone, he'll probably start to cry."

"No problem. Someone will feel sorry for him and take him home," I replied.

"But what will your mom say?" Cal asked.

I shrugged. "I'll tell her Vinnie ran off. I'll tell her we spent the whole night searching for him."

"Cool," Cal replied.

We led Vinnie to the haunted house at the dead end. It was old and creepy and surrounded by thick woods.

"We're not going to lock him in, are we?" Cal whispered.

"No. We'll just ditch him here," I whispered back. I turned to the mighty Darth Vader. "Go try this place," I said. I gave him a push into the weed-choked driveway.

The broken-down old house had no lights. I could barely see Vinnie step onto the front porch.

Cal and I took off, running as fast as we could.

We had only gone a few steps when we heard a frightening scream.

Vinnie!

Cal and I stopped. And listened.

We both gasped as we heard another shrill scream. Cut off in the middle.

And then . . . silence.

7

I laughed. "I guess poor old Vinnie met the ghost!" I exclaimed.

Cal glanced behind us toward the old house. "Shouldn't we go back and see if he's okay?"

"No way!" I cried. "He's fine. He just likes to scream. Besides, if something bad happened, it's too late anyway."

"But your mom —" Cal started.

"Forget about it," I replied. "Now that we ditched the losers, it's finally time for some fun."

I pulled the two rubber masks from my coat pocket and handed one to Cal. We both tugged our coats up over our heads and zipped them all the way. Then we propped the ugly masks on our shoulders.

"Headless Halloween!" I cried. "Come on. Let's find some victims!"

29

The block next to the middle school was crawling with trick-or-treaters. Cal and I waited behind a tall hedge.

When some kids came by, we jumped out in front of them and tugged off our masks.

"Headless Halloween!" Cal and I growled.

The kids screamed like crazy.

We made our way down the block, terrifying kids right and left. Without even trying, I made two little boys burst into tears.

A few minutes after that triumph, Cal and I jumped out into the street and made another boy fall off his bike.

Ha ha!

"I'm getting hungry," Cal said, his voice muffled under his coat.

"No problem," I replied.

I grabbed a full trick-or-treat bag from a kid wrapped from head to foot in mummy bandages. I knew that a mummy wouldn't be able to run after us very fast.

Cal and I took off across the street.

The kid was shrieking his head off. "Come back! That's mine! That's mine!"

I tossed him a Snickers bar. It bounced off his chest and into the street.

Then we ran until the little wimp was out of sight.

Cal and I hid behind someone's house. We dumped all the candy on the ground. Then we ripped open about a dozen candy bars and shoved them into our mouths.

Man, I *love* Halloween!

We heard the mummy boy crying his eyes out on the street. We pressed ourselves against the wall of the house and hid until the kid was gone.

Cal grinned. "Poor guy," he said. Cal had chocolate smeared all over his chin.

We stuffed ourselves with candy. I opened a bag of M&Ms, tilted it to my mouth, and poured them all down my throat.

Yum.

"Let's go," I said, burping up chocolate. "We've got to get to Mr. Benson's house — remember?"

"Are we just going to leave all this candy on the ground?" Cal asked, still chewing.

"No. Bring it with us," I replied. "We might get hungry while we're trashing Mountain's house."

"Cool," Cal said, swallowing a mouthful of Tootsie Rolls. He shoved a load of candy bars back into the bag.

Then we tucked our heads under our coats and walked headless up the hill toward Mr. Benson's house.

The moon had disappeared behind heavy black clouds. The houses ended as we neared Raven's Ravine, and the street grew very dark.

"Are we really going to trash Mountain's house?" Cal asked timidly.

"Sure," I replied, burping again. I didn't feel too well. Maybe I ate that candy too fast.

"Cool," Cal said. "But what if he's home?"

"We'll see," I murmured.

A few minutes later, Mr. Benson's house rose up over us. It stood in total darkness at the top of a steep hill. It reminded me of an evil castle, all stone, with tiny windows and a tall, round tower at one end.

I squinted past the house toward the ravine. Too dark to see anything back there.

"The house is dark," I said. "Maybe he went out."

"Maybe he just went to bed," Cal suggested.

We took a few steps up the front lawn. Then we both gasped as a side door swung open.

I ducked behind a tall evergreen shrub and pulled Cal beside me. Peering around the shrub, I saw Mr. Benson lumber out into the driveway. He tilted his head back, checking out the sky.

Then he disappeared into the stone garage to the right of the house. Cal and I ducked low behind the evergreen. A few seconds later, we heard a car engine start up. The teacher's black minivan backed down the drive and sped away.

I chuckled. "He *needs* a van. He doesn't fit in a car!"

Cal snickered too, his eyes on the old house. "Are we going in?"

"Why not?" I replied. "It's Halloween, isn't it? Time for a little Halloween mischief."

We stepped out from behind the shrub. Took two or three steps up the sloping lawn toward the house.

And stopped when we heard the angry growls.

"Dogs?" I choked out.

Yes.

Before Cal and I could move, two enormous, red-eyed dogs came charging at us, snarling furiously, heads lowered in attack.

oooooo!"

I let out a scream. Spun around. I tried to run — but I froze in fright.

Galloping hard, the dogs snarled in rage.

"We're . . . doomed," I muttered. I raised both hands to protect my face.

And heard a squeal. Two squeals. And a groan.

Lowering my hands, I gaped in surprise. The two attack dogs had stopped. They shook themselves, legs wobbling, dazed.

"They're tied up!" Cal cried, pointing. "See? They reached the end of their chains!"

My heart was pounding so hard, I could barely breathe. My stomach churned. I kept tasting chocolate.

I stared up the hill at the dogs.

They snarled down at us. But their hearts weren't in it. They knew they couldn't reach us. They knew they were defeated.

Cal and I burst out laughing. We slapped each other a few high fives. Then we made a big circle around the dogs and stepped up to the side door of the house.

Had Mr. Benson left it unlocked?

Yes.

The door creaked as I pushed it open. I led the way into the house.

"This is so cool," Cal whispered. "We are actually inside Mr. Benson's house!"

I waited for my eyes to adjust to the darkness. We stood in a long, narrow pantry. It smelled like pepper.

Walking slowly, carefully, we made our way into the kitchen.

Wind rustled the white curtains at the open window. Water dripped — *PLINK . . . PLINK . . .* — in the kitchen sink.

My stomach lurched, as if a wave crashed against the shore inside me. "I . . . I don't feel so well," I murmured.

I don't think Cal heard me. He had opened the refrigerator and was peering inside. "Wow! Mr. Benson drinks a *lot* of beer!" he exclaimed. "I guess that explains why he's so big!"

Laughing, Cal turned to me. I caught his excited expression in the light from the open refrigerator. "What are we going to do?" he asked. "Want to take all the food out of the fridge and throw it all over the house?"

I opened my mouth to answer. But my stomach heaved again.

"I feel sick. I — I'm going to hurl," I moaned.

I clapped my hand over my mouth.

Got to get to a bathroom, I told myself. Hurry. Get to a bathroom.

I started to the doorway. But then I had a better idea.

I turned and staggered to the kitchen table. Gripping the back of a chair, I leaned over — and threw up all over the checkered tablecloth.

I heaved up a lot. My whole dinner and all the candy I'd gobbled.

"Oooh, gross! Gross!" Cal groaned from across the kitchen.

When I finally finished, the kitchen table was practically covered. I had a sour taste in my mouth. But I felt a *lot* better.

I wiped my mouth with a corner of the tablecloth and stepped back.

Cal had a finger and thumb pressed over his nose. "You finished?" he asked.

I nodded weakly.

"Cool," he said. "I guess we don't have to do anything else."

I swallowed a couple of times, trying to get rid

of the bitter taste. "Huh? What do you mean?" I asked. My voice came out hoarse and scratchy.

"You left Mr. Benson a nice Halloween surprise," Cal replied, chuckling. "You redecorated his kitchen for him. I guess we can go now." He started to the side door.

"Whoa. Wait," I said, pulling him back. "Let's at least turn some furniture upside down or something."

Cal hesitated. "Yeah. Okay. That's cool."

"Let's turn the living room couch upside down," I suggested.

"And his TV set," Cal added.

"Awesome!" I was starting to feel a lot better.

But it didn't last.

We were in the hall nearly to the living room when I heard a door slam open.

"We're caught!" I gasped.

 heard a heavy *THUD* from the front.

"Quick!" I whispered. I grabbed Cal's sleeve and tugged him back through the hall.

"If he sees us, we're history!" Cal whispered, his eyes wide with fear.

We stumbled into the kitchen.

Behind us, I heard heavy breathing. The scrape of metal against the floor.

Metal?

Chains?

I jumped at the sound of a shrill bark.

"The dogs!" I cried.

I spun around in time to see the two attack dogs burst into the kitchen. Their chains scraped the floor behind them.

They both barked furiously now, lowering their heads menacingly, their eyes glowing red.

"They broke loose!" I cried.

My last words before both dogs leaped.

I ducked away. Then spun in panic.

Dove blindly for the open kitchen window — and shot headfirst ... out ... out into the cold night.

Gasping in deep breaths of fresh air, my chest heaving, I ran on trembling legs. I could hear the angry growls and cries of the dogs behind me from the kitchen.

Halfway across the backyard, halfway to the dark ravine up ahead, I turned back.

And saw Cal's head out the window. One arm stuck out. Flailing wildly.

"Hurry!" I cried.

But then I realized the big guy was stuck. Stuck in the narrow window.

"Help me!" His desperate shout was nearly drowned out by the fierce snarls of the attack dogs.

"Brandon — help!"

I took a step back toward the house — but stopped.

How could I help? What could I do for Cal now?

Run for it, Brandon, a voice inside my head urged.

You can't save Cal. Save yourself.

"Brandon — please!" Cal wailed. And then he let out a horrifying scream.

I swallowed hard. The dogs are chewing him to pieces, I realized.

And then I saw one of the dogs come running around the side of the house. Barking ferociously, it galloped across the yard toward me.

"Ohhh." I uttered a terrified moan. And spun away from the house — so hard I nearly fell.

And took off.

Running . . . running toward Raven's Ravine.

Panting, my heart thudding, I reached the edge of the ravine. The deep black hole opened in front of me.

I glanced back.

The barking dog was charging furiously, eyes blazing, teeth bared, its head lowered to the attack.

Only one way to escape. Jump the ravine!

I had only seconds.

I could see the other side of the ravine, only about ten feet away. And beneath me, a steep, steep drop — and then jagged, black rocks.

Could I jump it without a running start?

I had to try.

I glanced back to see the dog tilt back on its haunches. It uttered a howl as it prepared to attack.

I forced myself forward . . . bent my knees . . .

Tensed my leg muscles . . .

And jumped.

"Nooooo!" A terrified scream burst from my throat.

I missed.

Not far enough.
Not far enough . . .
My hands clawed the air. Nothing but air.
And then I was falling . . . falling so fast . . .
Falling to my death.

10

landed hard. Pain shot through my body. I shut my eyes, trying to squeeze away the pain.

When I opened my eyes, I gazed into heavy darkness. "Where am I?" I murmured, feeling dazed.

I couldn't see. Couldn't see a thing.

And then I realized my hands were clinging to the side of the ravine. My fingers dug into the dirt.

I made it.

Yes. I made it to the other side.

"Cal?" I murmured, still feeling dazed.

Did he make it out? Did he jump too?

"Ohhhhh," I moaned as the cold dirt crumbled. My fingers slid out.

I started to slide down the steep side of the ravine.

With a furious cry, I grasped the dirt. Dug my fingers in. Pulled myself up, my legs kicking and churning, my shoes scraping the side.

When I made it to the top, I dropped onto my stomach, arms outstretched on the cool dirt, hugging the ground.

It took a long time to catch my breath.

And then I pulled myself to my feet. And walked on trembling legs back to the edge of the ravine.

"Cal?" I called, cupping my hands around my mouth. "Cal? Are you there?"

I couldn't see him. Couldn't see the dog, either. Or the house beyond the backyard.

Too dark, I realized.

I brushed myself off and glanced around. I was beginning to feel a little more normal.

How do I get home from over here? I wondered. I realized I'd never been on this side of the ravine.

I turned and found myself facing a dark woods. Tall black trees rose up to the purple sky. The trees tilted in on each other, forming a fence.

Walking quickly, whistling to myself, I began following a twisting path through the woods.

I'm sure there are neighborhoods on the other side of the woods, I told myself. It's still pretty early. Probably lots of trick-or-treaters out.

The air grew colder as I stepped out of the woods. Zipping my coat up to my chin, I gazed around. I found myself on a narrow street with small, dark houses, very close together, on both sides.

No one on the street. No cars moving.

Where are the trick-or-treaters? I wondered.

I was starting to feel hungry. I'll scare the first kid I find and take his candy, I decided.

I pulled the rubber mask from my coat pocket and tugged it down over my head.

Now I just have to find someone to scare, I told myself. Where *is* everyone?

I walked along the sidewalk, peering over low bushes and hedges into dark front yards. I stopped at the first corner and squinted up at the street sign:

FIRST STREET.

"Never heard of it," I muttered.

The houses on the next block were even smaller, and very close together. Dim circles of yellow light from the streetlamps made my shadow stretch across the sidewalk. I couldn't see any other lights.

Still no people. No cars.

No dogs barking. No babies crying.

Nothing moved.

I whistled louder and scraped my shoes on the pavement, just to make a sound.

"Weird neighborhood," I muttered.

The next street sign read:

SECOND STREET.

I glanced around, trying to figure out in what direction I was heading. I knew I had to walk around the ravine and then back the way I'd come.

But which way was that?

Which way?

Peering into the darkness, I could no longer see the tall trees of the woods.

I'll try Second Street, I decided. I'll follow it until I come to some people. And then I'll ask directions.

Someone will know how I can get across the ravine and back to my neighborhood.

But Second Street was as empty and silent as the other street.

I tried humming a song, humming really loud, just to keep myself from totally losing it.

No wonder no one ever comes to this side of the ravine, I told myself. Everyone on this side must go to bed at eight o'clock!

And then I saw someone.

Down the street, about half a block away. Moving toward me on the sidewalk.

"Hey!" I called. "Hi!"

No reply.

I stopped walking and squinted into the dim yellow light. Was it a boy?

"Hi — I'm lost!" I called. "Can you help me?"

I took a few steps toward him. He kept walking, steadily, arms down at his sides.

And as he stepped under a streetlamp, I saw him clearly.

And gasped in shock.

The kid wore a mask. *My* mask.

The same ugly monster mask I had on.

Where did he get it? I wondered. I thought I had the only one like it.

He walked up to me, staring at me through the eye holes. He was about my height. Beneath the mask, he wore a faded denim jacket and baggy black jeans.

"Where did you get that mask?" I demanded.

He shrugged. "I don't remember."

"But it's the same as mine!" I exclaimed.

"Yeah." He stared at me, as if trying to recognize me.

"I — I'm lost," I stammered. "Where am I? I don't know this neighborhood."

"Well, how did you get here?" he asked.

"I . . . jumped the ravine," I told him. I laughed, a tense laugh. "A dog was chasing me. Do you believe it? So I jumped the ravine."

"Wow. That's really dangerous," he replied softly, his voice muffled behind the ugly mask.

"I guess," I murmured.

"Did you hear about the boy who tried to jump it and missed? He was crushed to death on the rocks."

"Yuck," I replied, feeling a chill. "I was lucky. I just made it to the other side."

"Yeah. Lucky," he repeated, still staring at me.

"You got any candy or anything?" I asked. "I'm really hungry."

He shook his head. "I didn't trick-or-treat. I'm going to a Halloween party. Over there." He pointed to a long, ranch-style house on the corner.

"How come it's so quiet over here?" I asked. "Where is everybody?"

"It's a quiet neighborhood," he replied. "Not many kids."

"And it's so dark," I added.

He snickered. "You're not afraid of the dark, are you?"

"No way," I replied quickly. "But I don't like being lost. Which direction is Main Street?"

"Over there, I think." He motioned with his head. "Want to come to the party?"

"A Halloween party?" I glanced at the house on

the corner. "How old are you? Halloween parties are kind of geeky, aren't they?"

"This one won't be," he replied softly. He turned and started walking toward the house.

I hurried after him. "Will there be food?"

"Yeah. Food. It's a party."

I trotted beside him. I thought we must look strange, both of us wearing the same creature mask. "What's your name?" I asked.

"Norband," he replied.

"Weird name," I muttered.

"Everyone calls me Norb," he said, walking faster.

"I'm Brandon," I said.

He stopped at the front steps and turned to me. "So are you coming to the party?"

"I guess," I replied. "For a little while. Then will you tell me how to get home?"

He didn't reply. Instead, he pushed open the front door and stepped into the house.

I followed him in. "Hey — it's totally dark in here!" I cried. "What's going on?"

12

Norb turned and stared at me through the mask. "What's your problem, Brandon?" he asked. "The party is downstairs, in the basement."

I felt like a jerk. As we moved through the house, I could hear music and voices from downstairs. Norb opened a door to the basement stairs, and the noise exploded over us.

"That better?" he asked.

"Yeah. Great," I replied. "Is this your house?"

Again, he didn't answer my question. He started down the steep stairs, taking them two at a time, motioning for me to follow.

As I made my way down, I saw bright, flashing lights, shadows dancing over the wall. And I heard kids laughing and talking, shouting over the steady boom of loud dance music.

At the bottom, I found myself in a large room, decorated for Halloween, with grinning, cardboard jack-o'-lanterns on the walls and orange and black crepe streamers hanging from the low ceiling.

The room was crowded with kids, at least thirty or forty boys and girls, all in masks and costumes. Some girls were dancing in the center of the room. Several boys watched, talking among themselves. Other kids clustered in small groups, talking and laughing. A couple of kids were wrapping themselves in orange crepe paper streamers.

"This is Brandon," Norb announced to a tall, skinny kid in a skeleton costume.

The skeleton nodded. "I'm Max."

"Brandon is hungry," Norb told him. Then he turned and started talking to two girls in witch costumes.

"The refreshment table is over here," Max said. He guided me past the dancing kids to a long table with an orange tablecloth. I saw piles of cookies and doughnuts, bowls of potato chips, and two half-eaten pumpkin pies.

"Give Brandon a doughnut," Norb instructed, suddenly appearing at the table.

"You like doughnuts?" Max asked.

I nodded. "Yeah. Sure. I'm suddenly starving."

He picked a doughnut off the top of the pile and handed it to me. He gazed through his skeleton mask, studying me. "These are special," he said.

"Thanks. Looks great," I said. I pulled off my mask.

Norb and Max crowded next to me as I raised the doughnut to my mouth. It was soft and doughy and covered with powdered sugar. My favorite.

I took a big bite. Chewed. Started to swallow.

And then groaned.

I felt something wet and warm on my tongue.

I raised the doughnut to examine it.

"Ohhhh." What was wriggling inside the doughnut?

Brown-and-purple worms!

I spit the wormy gob out.

Worms poked out from the doughnut. One crawled onto my hand.

With a cry of disgust, I started to toss the doughnut down.

But Norb grabbed my arm. He forced the doughnut to my face.

"Eat it, Brandon," he ordered. "Go on. Eat the whole thing."

"**N**o!" I struggled to pull my arm free.

But Max moved quickly to help Norb. The two of them held me in place — and shoved the disgusting doughnut into my face.

They forced the doughnut into my mouth.

I felt worms wriggle over my tongue and tickle the roof of my mouth.

I started to choke. But they pushed the doughnut in even farther.

"Chew! Chew it!" Norb ordered.

I had no choice. I didn't want to choke to death on a mouthful of worms. So I started to chew.

The sick, sour taste made me choke again.

My eyes were watering. I felt sweat roll down my forehead.

I shut my eyes and tried to pretend I was eating something else. Mashed potatoes.

But mashed potatoes don't squirm in your mouth!

I held my breath and swallowed. A thick chunk of worms slid down my throat.

Finally, I ate the whole thing.

Norb and his friend let go.

I staggered back against the food table, my chest heaving, my whole body shaking. The sour worm taste lingered in my mouth.

"Why?" I gasped. "Why did you *do* that?"

They both laughed behind their masks. "It's Halloween, isn't it?" Norb asked. He slapped Max a high five.

"Don't you like to do *scary* things on Halloween?" Max teased.

"That wasn't scary. That was sick," I grumbled angrily. "Bye. Thanks for nothing. I'm out of here."

I pushed past them and started toward the steps. But they grabbed me by the shoulders and pulled me back.

"You just got here," Norb said. His eyes flashed menacingly behind the mask.

"The party hasn't started yet," Max chimed in.

"Let go," I insisted. "Your party stinks."

But they squeezed my arms in a tighter grip.

"Hey, everyone," Norb shouted. "Hey, listen up! Brandon is going to bob for apples now!"

"I am not!" I protested. I squirmed and tugged. But they were stronger than me.

"Hey, everyone!" Norb shouted over the voices and the music. "Come watch. He's going to bob for apples!"

The two guys dragged me over to a big wooden barrel. I peered down. The barrel was filled with murky water, too dark to see anything.

Four or five kids came over to watch.

"Let go of me!" I shouted angrily. "I'm not dipping my head in there! There aren't even any apples in there!"

"Sure there are," Max replied. "Plenty of apples."

Norb grabbed the back of my neck and shoved my head down to the barrel. "Everyone bobs for apples at a Halloween party," he said softly.

"What are you trying to prove?" I cried. "Get away from me! Are you crazy? Let me go!"

I stared down at the dark water. "I don't see any apples!"

"Look closer," Norb replied.

They held me and pushed my head lower. My nose and cheeks splashed into the disgusting water.

Sputtering, I forced my head up. "Why are you doing this?" I gasped.

"It's a Halloween party," Norb insisted.

"Go ahead, Brandon," Max urged. "Grab an apple in your teeth, and you're finished."

"I just want to get out —" I started.

But they shoved my head into the barrel again.

They're *sick*, I told myself. They're totally messed up.

I'll grab an apple. Then I'm out of here.

I opened my eyes. But I couldn't see anything in the thick, murky water.

Something prickled my face. I felt something soft and wet crawl into my ear.

Sputtering, I tried to pull my head out. But Max and Norb held me down, pushing me deeper into the barrel.

I felt something scrape against my cheek. The back of my neck tingled as tiny creatures crawled over it. My whole face prickled.

With a surge of power, I forced my head up. I stared into the barrel.

The dark water churned and rolled. Alive!

The water was alive!

No. Not water . . . Not water . . .

I stared into a tossing, churning pile of *cockroaches*!

Before I could sputter a protest, they pushed my head back into the pile.

I gasped in horror as cockroaches scrabbled over my face, dug into my hair, climbed into my nose and ears.

I struggled to pull away. But the boys held my arms down as they pressed me into the barrel.

I opened my mouth to scream — and felt cockroaches slide into my mouth, crawl over my tongue.

I — I swallowed them!

"That doesn't count. Grab one!" I heard Norb urge behind me. "Bite it! Bite it!"

"Grab one! Get one!" Max shouted.

I heard kids cheering and laughing.

My stomach lurched. I'm going to be sick, I realized.

Cockroaches swarmed over my face, my hair.

"Grab one! Grab one!" kids chanted.

I can't take this, I realized. I can't take this anymore.

I've got to end it. Got to stop it . . .

No choice. I don't have a choice.

I shut my eyes and opened my mouth wide.

And grabbed a bunch of cockroaches between my teeth.

14

chomped down and raised my head. I could feel the sticky insects between my teeth, on my tongue.

With a groan, I opened my mouth and began to spit. I spit the cockroaches back into the barrel. I kept spitting after they were all out of my mouth, trying to get rid of the sour taste, the horrible tickling.

Kids laughed and clapped. Norb slapped me hard on the back. "Scary enough for you, Brandon?" he demanded. His eyes flashed gleefully behind his mask.

"Let's get scary!" someone called out. And the others began to chant: "Let's get scary! Let's get scary!"

This is a *nightmare*! I thought.

This can't be happening to me. These kids are *evil!*

"Can I go now?" I asked Norb. My voice trembled. I pulled cockroach legs off my tongue.

He didn't answer, so I tried again. "I'm out of here," I said. "You can't keep me here."

"Sure, we can," Norb replied. He motioned with both hands, and several costumed kids circled me.

"Let's get scary," they chanted. "Let's get scary!"

Norb squeezed my shoulder until I cried out. "Let's play a game," he said. "Everyone plays games at a party — right, Brandon?"

"I want to go," I said through gritted teeth. "You can't keep me here. It's . . . *kidnapping!*"

For some reason, that got a big laugh from everyone.

"I mean it!" I screamed. "Let me out of here!"

"How about Twister?" Norb demanded, ignoring my pleas. "You like to play Twister?"

"No!" I replied angrily. "No games. I want out!"

Norb dug his fingers into my shoulder. "Okay. Twister," he said softly. He pulled me into the center of the room. "Are you having fun, Brandon? Is it scary enough for you?"

I tugged hard. Tried to break free.

But his hand clamped down on my shoulder, sending pain shooting through my whole body. He

59

gave me a hard shove — and I stumbled forward to the edge of a Twister mat on the floor.

"You go first," he ordered.

"I won't play!" I crossed my arms in front of my chest. "No way."

Kids surrounded me. Norb's dark eyes glared at me through the eyeholes of his mask. "You'd better enjoy this part, Brandon," he said softly. "This is the fun part. After this, it gets *really* scary."

"Huh? Why?" I cried. "What do you mean?"

He didn't reply.

"What comes next?" I demanded. "What are you going to *do* to me?"

15

 few seconds later, I was down on my hands and knees on the mat. A boy in a vampire costume was draped over my back, also on his hands and knees.

Who are these kids? I wondered, my heart pounding.

Why are they doing this to me?

Is this just their idea of Halloween fun? Or are they really evil?

The boy in the vampire costume shifted his weight on top of me.

All around me, kids were chanting: "Let's get scary! Let's get scary!" Their voices echoed off the basement walls, ringing louder and louder in my ears.

"Let's get scary! Let's get scary!"

I shivered.

Were they going to let me go? Or did they plan to torture me all night?

I didn't have long to think about it.

A girl in a monkey costume plopped down onto the mat beside me and wrapped an arm around my arm.

"I don't want to play," I groaned. "Get off! Get off me!"

I felt another arm twist around my legs.

The boy on my back began to feel heavier. An arm twisted around my other arm.

"I *hate* this game!" I shrieked. "Why are you doing this to me?"

The vampire boy suddenly felt lighter. Was he getting up?

I heard a loud *HISSSSS*, close to my ear.

Turning my head, I saw the arm tangled around my arm . . . saw it begin to change . . . to grow slimmer . . . to curl itself tighter around me . . .

Another *HISSSSS*. So close. So close.

And then the *SNAP* of jaws.

Something coiled around my waist. And tight-ened . . . tightened.

Snakes.

The kids were shrinking . . . changing . . . chang-ing into snakes.

They curled around me. Around my chest, my arms, my legs.

"Noooooo!" A moan of horror escaped my throat.

A loud *SNAP* at my ear made me gasp. Scratchy, warm skin slid around my neck.

And now they were all hissing. Tightening themselves around my neck. Hissing. Snapping.

I'm ... suffocating, I realized.

Can't breathe ... Can't breathe.

I dropped facedown, flat against the mat. With a desperate lunge, I rolled onto my back.

I tossed one arm — and flung one snake off.

Then I reached up. Grabbed the snake around my neck — and pulled it off.

It twisted in my hand. Shot its head forward. Snapped its jaws close to my face, so close I felt its hot breath on my cheek.

With a wild heave, I sent it flying into the crowd of chanting kids.

Then, pulling another snake from around an ankle, I jumped to my feet.

The room spun. I blinked several times, struggling to steady myself.

The kids stood in a circle around me, chanting, their voices muffled and strange behind their masks. Clapping their hands in a slow, steady rhythm. Repeating their frightening words over and over.

"Let's get scary ... Let's get scary!"

I've got to get away from here, I told myself.

I have to escape. While I still can.

But how?

I glanced frantically around the room. The

orange and black streamers shimmered, twisting down from the ceiling like snakes.

And beyond them . . . Beyond them, I saw the basement stairs. And the door at the top of the stairs.

Open.

The door stood open.

Could I make a run for it? Could I reach the door and run out of this house, away from these weird, chanting kids?

I knew I had to try.

I took a step. Then another.

And then Norb's hand grasped my shoulder again. His eyes peered into mine. "Are you ready for a real Halloween trick?" he asked. "I'm going to make you disappear."

16

"**N**oooo!" I let out an angry shriek.

Then I grabbed Norb's wrist with both hands — and swung his hand off my shoulder.

Behind the ugly mask, his eyes bulged in surprise.

I didn't give him a chance to grab me again. I spun away and dove into the crowd of kids. Lowering my head like a fullback, I bulled right through them.

The chanting stopped. Startled cries rang out.

My head down, I ran without looking back. Ran through the forest of streamers. Ran to the stairs, my eyes on the open door.

"Owwww!"

I stumbled at the bottom step. Banged my knee. Pain shot up my body.

But I grabbed the banister and pulled myself up.

Up the stairs, trying to ignore my throbbing knee. Up the stairs. The open door so close now.

"Yes!" I uttered a happy cry as I reached the top and burst through the doorway. I could hear the cries and shouts below, distant now.

I glanced down for a second. They weren't chasing after me.

Breathing a long sigh, I spun away and plunged through the dark house. Out the front door and down the front lawn to the street.

My shoes slid on the dew-covered grass.

I ran through total darkness. No moon. No stars. No streetlamps or lights from any houses.

Black trees swayed silently against a charcoal sky.

Nothing else moved. No cars rolled by. No one else out on the street.

I crossed a street and kept running. I had no idea what direction I was headed. I had to get away, as far away from that house and those kids as I could.

I ran till a sharp pain in my side slowed me to a trot.

The houses ended, and I found myself moving between heavily wooded lots. As I followed the curve of the road, pale light washed over the ground, over the sidewalk, over me.

I gazed up to see the moon slide out from behind

the clouds. The silvery moonlight made the tall trees shimmer, unreal and ghostlike.

My shoes thudded the pavement. I was breathing hard as I jogged, my heart pounding, my side still aching.

Where *was* everyone?

How could I be the only person out on Halloween night in this neighborhood?

I stopped when I saw something move in the grass of an empty lot. I narrowed my eyes, struggling to see clearly.

A dog? A rabbit standing tall among the weeds?

I took a step closer.

Something poked up from the grass, moving slowly, waving like a small tree, reaching toward the sky.

Something . . .

"Oh, no!" I moaned. "Oh, nooooo!"

17

A hand!
A human hand.
I swallowed hard, staring in disbelief. Beside it, another hand poked up from beneath the ground. It shook itself, shaking dirt off.

Both hands reached up, making grasping motions, curling and uncurling fingers.

Frozen in silence, I squinted into the eerie, pale light. And watched more hands pop up from beneath the ground.

They shook off dirt and stretched. Bony arms stretched up from the grass. The hands opened and closed. The fingers curled and made grabbing motions.

A dozen hands poked up. Now a dozen more, shimmering yellow and green in the moonlight.

Hands reaching up from the ground. Grabbing, grabbing at air. Pushing the dirt aside . . . stretching . . . stretching . . .

And then heads. Human heads. Hair caked with dirt. Skin loose, hanging from their skulls.

Head after head poked up from the dirt.

They stared at me with pleading eyes, faces twisted, mouths hanging open as if in pain.

"Take me with you," one of them called in a dry whisper.

"No. Take me!" another croaked.

"Take me with you. Take me with you." The chant went up.

And they reached for me — all of them — reaching from under the dirt, hands curling and uncurling, eyes, vacant sunken eyes, pleading, pleading.

"Take me with you."

How can this be happening? How can dead people poke up from the dirt? Were they really dead? What was going on here? I wondered.

I shut my eyes. Forced myself to spin away from the ugly, frightening sight.

And then, with a lurching start, I ran. Ran full speed, leaning forward, my arms outstretched.

My legs felt wobbly and weak. My throat tightened until my breath escaped in wheezing gasps.

But I ran, ran blindly, ran without slowing. Followed the curving path through the trees.

And then stopped with a cry as the trees ended.

As the *ground* ended.

And I stared at a deep gash in the ground. A break. A split in the earth.

The ravine?

Yes!

I had found it. I had returned to it.

Raven's Ravine stretched darkly in front of me.

"Oh, thank goodness," I sighed.

I bent forward, lowering my hands to my knees. And waited to catch my breath. Waited for my head to stop spinning, for my temples to stop throbbing.

I stood there hunched over for a minute, maybe two. Breathing . . . breathing . . . and staring at the narrow ravine.

I jumped it once, I told myself. I can jump it again.

And then I'll be home. Then I'll be away from this empty, frightening place.

Finally starting to feel normal, I stood up straight. And stepped to the edge of the ravine.

"No problem," I murmured. "I can jump this easily."

I lowered my gaze down the side of the steep cliff to the dark rocks below.

And cried out when I saw a body. A boy — sprawled at the bottom. Lying on his stomach. Arms and feet spread over the rocks as if hugging them.

70

Cal?

Cal?

My whole body trembling, I dropped to my knees. Leaned over the side to see better.

Cal?

Cal must have followed me out of Mr. Benson's house. He must have tried to jump the ravine too.

And missed. Missed.

And now my friend — my best friend — lay there, crushed, stretched out over the rocks, lifeless and unmoving.

"Cal?" I called down to him, my voice hoarse and trembling.

"Cal? Are you alive? Can you hear me?"

No.

"Cal? Can you move? Can you —"

Whoa.

Wait.

I grasped the dirt edge of the ravine and leaned farther over the side. Leaned until I nearly fell in.

"Cal?"

No.

Not Cal.

Squinting hard, leaning as far as I could, I saw that it wasn't Cal sprawled on the rocks below.

Not Cal. Not Cal. Not Cal.

It was *me*.

18

"Hunnnnh?"

My breath burst from my chest like an explosion.

My whole body lurched from the shock.

And before I could pull back from the edge, I started to fall.

As I toppled forward, strong hands grabbed my shoulders. Someone pulled me back. Hoisted me back onto solid ground. And flung me — flung me with incredible strength — onto my back.

Whimpering in shock, my chest heaving up and down, I stared up at Norb.

"Problem?" he asked calmly, eyeing me through the ugly mask.

Over his shoulder, I saw the others appear. Max in his skeleton costume, the vampire, the girl dressed as a monkey. Still in costume, they stepped out of the woods and made their way to the ravine's edge.

I forced myself to sit up. "What . . ." I choked out. I couldn't finish my thought.

They all laughed. Norb stood over me, hands on his waist.

I tried again. "What . . . happened?"

Norb shook his head. "Brandon, don't you get it?"

"No," I told him. "What is happening? Down there . . ." I pointed to the ravine.

"It's you," he said flatly.

"I know. But —" I swallowed.

"You didn't make it," he said softly.

"Huh?"

"You tried to jump the ravine, and you didn't make it." He hunched down next to me. "Try to remember."

"I — I can't," I stammered. "I jumped and . . ." I thought hard. I remembered landing hard . . . everything going dark.

Was it true?

I didn't make it across the ravine?

"You died," Norb said flatly, with no emotion at all. "Your body died down there, Brandon. But your spirit made it to the other side."

"The other side," a girl murmured.

"The other side . . . The other side . . ."

"My *spirit*?" I gasped.

Norb nodded. "You've joined us on the other side."

"No. No way," I murmured weakly. I shook my head. "I don't believe it."

"You're with us now, Brandon," Norb repeated. "You will stay with us on the other side."

"Forever," the skeleton chimed in.

"Forever," a girl repeated.

"No!" I protested. I grabbed the front of Norb's jacket with both hands. "No!" I cried. "You've got to let me go. Please — let me go!"

He shook his head. "Can't."

"I promise I'll be good. I'll never scare anyone again! Promise!" I wailed.

They all laughed. Cold, scornful laughter.

"Can't do," Norb said softly.

He brushed my hands away. "You're frightened — aren't you?" he demanded.

"Yes," I confessed. "I'm frightened."

"Now you know what it feels like," he replied. "Now you're on the other end. You know what it feels like to be really scared."

"I promise I'll never frighten anyone again!" I cried. "Listen to me. I promise —"

The others burst into laughter once more.

I couldn't resist looking again. My legs trembling, I crawled back to the ravine's edge — and peered down.

Peered down at my own body. Stretched over the rocks. So still. So horribly still.

"What can I do?" I demanded, turning back to Norb. "There has to be something I can do to get back."

He stared at me for what seemed like hours. "Maybe . . ." he said finally.

"Tell me!" I screamed. "Please — I'm begging you! I can't stay here on the other side! I have to go back! Tell me what I can do!"

Norb's eyes flashed behind the mask. "There's only one way," he said.

19

"What?" I scrambled over to him and grabbed his jacket again. "Tell me what I have to do. I'll do anything!"

"It won't be easy — for you," Norb replied.

"I'll do it," I promised. "Whatever it is."

"You have to help people," he said.

"Huh?" I waited desperately for him to continue.

A gust of cold air swirled around us. A clump of dirt broke off the edge of the ravine and tumbled to the rocks below.

A picture flashed into my mind. A terrifying picture. I saw myself falling down to the rocks, falling like a clump of dirt.

"You have to help people who are frightened," Norb continued finally. "You have to rescue them.

76

Three people. You have to find three frightened people and help them."

I stared at him. "Is that all?"

He nodded. "It won't be easy," he said again, his voice just above a whisper.

"I can do it," I vowed. "And after I do it . . . ?"

"You can stay on your side," he replied. "You can go back to your life."

"Th-thanks," I stammered. "I —"

"Don't thank me," Norb replied coldly. "If you fail, you won't feel like thanking me. If you fail, you will never see your family or friends again. You will stay with us on the other side."

"I won't fail," I told him.

He snickered. "Oh, yeah?" he sneered. "Oh, yeah? We'll see about that."

And then he shot up both arms — and gave me a hard shove over the side of the ravine.

20

I screamed all the way down.

I landed on my side on the sharp, jagged rocks at the bottom of the ravine. Bounced once. Then lay still.

I shut my eyes and waited for the crushing pain.

But to my surprise, I felt nothing.

I opened my eyes, my heart still pounding in my chest. And stared at the body sprawled facedown on the rocks beside me.

My body.

I grabbed it by the shoulders and turned it over.

A wave of nausea rolled over me. I couldn't bear to look at myself. I let go of the body. It fell back onto the rocks with a soft *PLOP*.

I'm dead, I thought, hugging myself, struggling to fight down the nausea.

I'm really dead.

How can I help people without my body? I wondered.

How can I rescue three frightened people if I'm a ghost?

I need my body, I told myself. If I'm a ghost, I'll terrify people. I won't be able to help them.

I raised my eyes to the top of the ravine. "Hey!" I called up. "Are you still there? Norb? Are you up there?"

No reply.

I heard giggling, hushed whispers.

I cupped my hands around my mouth and shouted. "I can hear you. I know you're up there!"

Finally, Norb's masked face appeared over the cliff's edge. "What do you want, Brandon? Do I have to give you another push to get you started?"

More giggling behind him.

"I need my body!" I cried. "How can I help anyone without my body?"

Norb frowned down at me. "You can have it back for one hour," he announced.

"Only one hour? But — but —" I sputtered.

"Yes. You have only one hour. One hour to save three frightened people."

"And if I can't do it in one hour?" I asked in a trembling voice.

No reply.

Norb vanished from view. Silence up there now.

It didn't matter. I knew the answer to my question.

If I didn't rescue three people in one hour, I'd return to the other side. And stay there . . . forever.

But how do I get my body back? I wondered.

"Norb, I need your help," I shouted. "How do I —"

Suddenly I felt so warm, so snug.

I gazed down at the ground — my body wasn't there.

I'm back to being me! I realized. I'm not dead anymore.

I stood up and tested it. Wriggled my hands. Bent my knees. I coughed. Laughed. Shook my whole body.

It felt so wonderful to be *me* again!

"Only one hour," I reminded myself.

I stepped up to the cliff wall, dug my hands into the hard, rocky dirt, and started to pull myself up to the top.

I was about halfway up when I heard the furious animal snarls.

The snarls became an angry howl.

My heart stopped. I clung to the side of the ravine.

Two animals now, growling furiously.

I recognized the sound. Mr. Benson's attack dogs.

Were they waiting for me at the top?

I pulled myself up higher. My legs trembled so hard, I nearly toppled back down.

Above me, the dogs growled and barked angrily. Darkness rolled over me as the moon vanished behind clouds once again.

Rocks crumbled at my feet and fell to the ravine's bottom. I heard them hit the ground below. And again, I pictured myself falling, falling to my death.

I shook away the image and I forced myself to the top.

The shrill howls of the dogs sent chill after chill down my back. I stepped onto the flat ground — and prepared myself for their attack.

No.

No dogs waiting. No dogs tensed for attack at the ravine's edge.

Mr. Benson's old house rose up darkly in front of me. The angry dogs were inside.

Above their howls, I heard a terrified cry. A human cry.

Cal?

Was Cal still in the house? Did time stand still while I was on the other side?

I lurched across the backyard, my shoes slipping on the frosty, wet grass.

Another hoarse cry of terror floated out from the open kitchen window.

Yes. Cal.

I recognized Cal's voice.

I dove to the window. Leaned over the ledge and peered into the dark house.

The two sleek gray dogs, snarling and barking, had Cal backed into a corner. He had his hands raised in front of him, as if trying to shield himself.

The dogs bared their teeth. One of them angled back on its haunches, preparing to leap.

Cal lowered his hands. His eyes met mine.

"Brandon!" he gasped. "Where did you go? Help me! Hurry!"

I lifted myself over the window ledge.

"Help me!" Cal pleaded. "They're going to tear me to pieces!"

I landed hard on my feet on the kitchen floor. "What can I do?" I cried.

"Get them off! Get them away!" Cal shrieked.

"I — I'll try!" I stammered.

I took a few steps toward the angry dogs.

One of them turned and bared its teeth at me, a deep growl bursting from its throat.

And then the other one swung around, its eyes glowing red. Both dogs studied me now. Cal stayed pressed in the corner, his big chest heaving up and down, his arms still raised as a shield.

Low, menacing growls from both dogs.

"Whoa —" I murmured.

They moved quickly.

Lowering their heads, they shot across the room — and sprang at me!

22

tried to duck under them.

Too late.

Heavy paws hit me hard. My chest. My shoulder.

I staggered back against the sink.

And howled in pain as one of the snarling creatures sank its teeth into my ankle.

As I slid to the floor, I glimpsed Cal frozen in the corner, his eyes wide with fright.

"Run!" I screamed. "Get *out* of here! Go!"

A dog leaped at me again. Pushed me onto my back on the floor. The other dog tore at my jeans cuff.

"Get out of here!" I shouted again.

Finally, Cal moved. He took a few unsteady steps toward the back door.

"*Go!*" I shrieked as both dogs tore at me with their teeth.

"B-But . . . you?" Cal stammered.

"Don't worry about me!" I cried. "You can't help me! Get out! Out!"

He hesitated another second. "I'll get help," he said.

He shoved open the back door with both hands and disappeared outside.

A dog paw slashed across my face. Twisting and pulling, the other dog tore at my jeans.

Gasping, I struggled to wrestle free.

They won't stop until they've torn me apart, I realized. I'll never be able to save anyone!

I've got to get them off me. I have to find a way to distract them.

I kicked out at the snarling dog at my feet.

It uttered an enraged howl — and dug its teeth harder into my jeans leg. Over my gasping breaths, I heard a loud *RRRIP* as the creature pulled the jeans apart.

The other dog stood on my chest, pinning me to the floor.

How can I distract them? I asked myself. How?

And then I spotted the trick-or-treat bag on the kitchen counter. The bag Cal and I had taken from the little kid.

There was still some candy in the bag, I remembered.

And dogs like candy — right?

In my panic, my mind whirred from thought to thought.

Get the bag to the dogs. Show the candy to them.

Maybe ... maybe they'll go for the candy. Maybe they'll let go long enough for me to escape.

The kitchen counter stood in the middle of the room. Miles away ...

With a groan, I shoved the big dog off my chest. I rolled onto my side.

Then I kicked out hard with both legs. Kicked the other dog off me. It tilted up its head, roaring in rage.

I rolled again. Jumped to my feet.

Dove for the counter.

Yes. Yes!

I grabbed the bag in both hands — and heaved it to the floor.

The bag landed on its side. Candy bars rolled onto the floor.

Would the dogs go for it? Would they go for the candy?

I stared at the floor as they approached it. Sniffed it.

No. No. No ...

Snarling furiously, they stepped over the candy — and bared their teeth, red eyes glowing, preparing to attack me again.

23

"Nooooo!" I let out a howl of terror.

As the dogs leaped, I dove to the floor. I grabbed a candy bar in each hand.

And tossed them in the air.

I rolled away as both dogs jumped up, snapping their jaws at the flying candy.

The dogs caught the candy bars in their teeth. They finally stopped growling as they bit down. Started to chew.

Yes!

I saw my chance. I bolted for the open door. As I ran, I scooped two more candy bars off the floor and tossed them to the dogs.

"Trick or treat, guys!" I choked out.

And then I was gone. Out the door and running full speed around the side of the house.

"Cal?" I called to him as I burst down the steeply sloping front lawn. "Cal? Are you still here?"

I didn't see him.

I didn't stop running. I raced into the street, glancing back to see if the dogs were coming after me.

No. Not yet.

I turned and ran down the block. Crossed a street. And kept running.

One down, I thought. One frightened person saved.

How much time do I have left?

I stopped beneath a streetlamp to check my watch. I raised it to my eyes and stared.

"Oh, no." A sigh escaped my throat as I saw that my watch had stopped. The second hand stood frozen at twelve.

I shook the watch. Pounded it against my wrist. It wouldn't move.

Did the watch break when I fell down the ravine? I wondered. Or did time stop when I died?

No time to think about it. I had to save two more people. And I had to do it fast.

I saw a group of costumed kids running eagerly to a house across the street. They were laughing and joking with each other. One boy was stuffing his face with candy — right through a monster mask.

Kids having fun, I thought sadly.

They rang the doorbell and yelled, "Trick or treat!" Watching them, I wondered if I would ever have fun again. If I would ever be normal again. If I would ever be alive . . .

A wave of despair washed over me. I can't do this, I decided. I might as well give up now.

Where will I even find frightened people I can help?

It's Halloween night. Everyone is out having fun. No one is in trouble.

Two kids in vampire costumes came roaring by on bikes, their capes flying up behind them. I jumped into a hedge to get out of their way.

They laughed and kept pedaling hard.

I shook my head sadly. I'll go home, I decided. I'll take one last look at my house. At my family.

I don't know how much time I have left. Probably just enough time to say good-bye.

I trudged around the corner and started down the next block. Lost in my sad thoughts, I didn't pay much attention to the houses and yards I passed.

Glancing up, I found myself at a dead end. Woods stretched in both directions. A dark, old house loomed between tangled trees.

The haunted house!

The house where Cal and I had abandoned Vinnie.

I stepped into the tall weeds at the front of the yard. And peered up at the house.

Dark and silent.

A windowpane was missing in an upstairs window. The wind blew in, fluttering dark curtains.

A TV antenna tilted over the roof like a broken bird. Part of the chimney had crumbled away, leaving bricks scattered over the driveway.

Did something move in the front window? Did I see a flash of light? A face?

"Vinnie." I murmured his name.

Cal and I heard him scream, I remembered. But we left him there anyway. We left him there and ran away.

Was Vinnie still here? Still in this frightening house?

I had to find out. I stepped through the tall weeds, making my way to the front door.

The house had been empty for years. Clumps of grass and weeds rose up nearly to my waist. I stumbled over rocks and old bottles and other junk.

All the neighborhood kids believed the house was haunted. Some of them said they saw strange, shimmering lights in the house late at night. Kids claimed they heard howls and moans that couldn't be made by humans.

Cal and I always had so much fun locking kids in the house. Were they scared? Some of them still haven't stopped screaming!

That was back in the days when things were

still funny. Now, as I approached the house, I remembered the fun we had — but I didn't laugh.

"Vinnie?" I called. My voice came out muffled, soft.

I stepped onto the rotting porch. The damp floorboards creaked and sank under my shoes. "Vinnie?"

I heard something from inside. A moan? A cry?

I took a deep breath and pushed open the front door.

The attack came so fast, I couldn't even scream.

24

I heard a *SCREE SCREE SCREE*.

Something hit my forehead and bounced off.

Stunned, I stumbled back onto the porch.

I rubbed my head and heard frantic fluttering.

Shadows — many shadows — flew over me.

Bats!

Were they attacking?

Blinking away the pain, I heard the *SCREE SCREE* again. The fluttering sounds had moved to the trees.

I waited for a moment, catching my breath. Then I peered cautiously through the front doorway. The house seemed empty now.

The front room stood dark. I couldn't see a thing.

Holding on to the door frame, I stepped inside.

"Vinnie?" I called in a choked whisper. I cleared my throat and called again. "Vinnie — are you here?"

"Brandon?"

My name floated to me, weak and hoarse, from somewhere deep in the house.

"Brandon — is that you?"

My eyes adjusted slowly to the darkness. I followed the sound of Vinnie's voice, through a long, dark hallway that led straight back.

"Vinnie — where are you?" I called. My words echoed down the long hall.

"I'm back here," came his reply. "But don't come in. Don't come in, Brandon!"

"Huh?" I let out a startled gasp.

"Get away as fast as you can!" Vinnie warned in a trembling, little voice. "It — it's so big, Brandon. And so ugly."

I stopped at a closed door at the end of the hall. "What is big?" I called in.

"Go away!" Vinnie cried from the other side of the door. "It's too late for me. But you can still escape."

I raised my hand to the cold doorknob. "Escape from what, Vinnie?" I demanded.

I waited. A shiver ran down my back. A gust of cold air from somewhere in the house chilled me all over.

"Vinnie?" I called in.

I waited again. Then I turned the knob and

pushed in the door. I stepped into a dark room cluttered with old furniture. Couches and tall chairs, most of them covered in sheets and blankets.

I blinked in the gray light.

"Don't —" Vinnie cried.

He sat hunched on a tall, stiff wooden chair.

I squinted to see if he was tied down. No. Nothing holding him there.

"Come on," I urged, waving him over to me. "Let's get out of here."

"I . . . can't," he choked out. His face was twisted in fright. He had chewed his bottom lip until it bled.

"Hurry. Come with me!" I cried.

"I can't!" he cried. "It . . . won't let me leave."

"There's nothing here," I argued. "The house is empty. Come on, Vinnie —"

"It's here!" he whimpered. "It's a ghost. The stories are true, Brandon. Only, it's more horrible than you can imagine. It's not like a movie ghost. It —"

He stopped short, and his eyes bulged with fright. He raised a trembling finger to his lips.

I listened. And I heard it.

I heard heavy, rhythmic thuds from behind me in the long hall. Echoing thuds.

Such heavy, steady footsteps.

Closer . . . closer.

"Get away," Vinnie moaned. He clasped and unclasped his hands. "Hurry, Brandon."

"Not without you," I told him.

The footsteps thudded in my ears.

"No. Run — before it's too late!" Vinnie cried in a terrified whisper.

A heavy thud made me spin around.

It *was* too late!

innie didn't move. He sat hunched in the stiff chair, trembling, his hands tightly clasped.

THUD. THUD.

Heavy footsteps made the floorboards creak.

I dove behind a couch and dropped to my hands and knees.

"Vinnie — hide!" I whispered.

He didn't move.

My hand bumped something hard and cold. I gasped.

Only a flashlight.

I rolled it out of my way and peered out from behind the couch.

And stared at a ghost.

A man. A very large man. Dressed in a loosely

flowing robe. All gray from head to foot. No color. Gray hair, gray eyes, gray skin, gray robe.

Gray bare feet slapped the floor as he moved across the room. *THUD. THUD.*

I froze behind the couch, gaping in amazement. And as the gray ghost moved closer, I saw that his head was split. Split in half, right down the middle. As if a hatchet had sliced his skull.

The gray eyes rolled wildly on each side of the crack. His nose was split in two. The crack ran down past his lips and stopped at his chin.

As he stepped into the gray light and lowered his head toward Vinnie, I could see inside his skull.

I could see gray brains, bubbling, bubbling inside the opening in the skull.

His belly bouncing beneath the robe, the huge, ugly ghost lowered his cracked head. Brought his face close to Vinnie.

What is he going to do? I wondered.

I have to save Vinnie. I have to frighten away that ghost.

But how?

On my hands and knees behind the couch, I watched the ghost lower his face to Vinnie. "Unh . . . unh . . ." The split lips opened in a low grunt. "Unh . . ."

Vinnie whimpered in terror. He sat trembling on the chair. Staring straight ahead.

Suddenly, I had an idea. A desperate idea.

Maybe a stupid idea. But the only idea I had.

I'll try going headless, I decided. I'll pop out headless and rush at the big ghost. Maybe . . . just maybe, it will startle the ghost long enough for me to pull Vinnie away.

I sat down on the floor. My hands trembling, I pulled my coat up over my head and zipped it all the way.

I hesitated. If this doesn't work, I thought, I might be headless forever.

My head was hidden beneath my coat. I couldn't see a thing.

But I didn't need to see. I could hear the ghost's disgusting grunts. I knew where it was standing.

I took a deep breath.

Then I jumped to my feet, shot my arms out at my sides, and burst out headless into the room, shrieking as I ran.

y cry echoed off the walls.

Halfway across the room, I shot my head up through the top of the coat to see.

The gray ghost stared at me, his split mouth open. On both sides of the deep rut down his face, his gray eyes bulged.

He tossed back his ugly head and uttered a cry of his own.

And then he raised his hands to his jaw — and tugged the head off his shoulders.

The head screamed. The eyes rolled crazily.

Holding the screaming head in both hands, the ghost raised it high over his shoulders.

I staggered back. Whimpering in terror, Vinnie covered his face with his hands.

Another shrill scream escaped the ghost's head.

And then to my shock, the big ghost turned away from us. Turned heavily. And still holding up its screaming head, it staggered away.

It staggered heavily to the door. And disappeared into the long hallway.

I could hear the screams ringing through the hall, growing fainter and fainter as the ghost retreated.

"Vinnie —" I gasped, diving to his chair. "Vinnie — I did it! I scared him away!"

"No," he murmured. He still had his face buried in his hands. "No, you don't understand."

"Huh? Let's go!" I urged, tugging Vinnie's arm. "Open your eyes! Get up! Let's go! I scared away the ghost!"

"No," Vinnie said, finally lowering his hands. "No, Brandon." He shook his head. "You don't understand. That wasn't the ghost."

"Huh?" I stared at him, totally confused.

"That wasn't the ghost," Vinnie repeated. "That was the ghost's *pet!*"

27

y mouth dropped open. I stared at my cousin, trying to make sense of his words. "P-pet?" I stammered.

Vinnie nodded, his face so pale and twisted in fear.

"Well, then . . . where is the ghost?" I asked.

Before Vinnie could answer, I felt something move.

The floor.

The floor curled beneath my feet.

I heard a loud rumble — and the walls began to slide in — to close in on us.

"What's going on?" I cried.

"Don't you see?" Vinnie wailed. "The *whole house* is the ghost! The *whole house* is evil. It — it's been holding me here! It won't let me move!"

"Let's get out of here!" I started toward Vinnie. Reached out to pull him from his chair — and the floor buckled.

I stumbled. Then fell to my knees as the floor turned soft. It seemed to melt under my feet.

"I don't think I can make it over to you!" I cried.

"Don't try, Brandon. It's useless. We're doomed!" Vinnie wailed.

I crawled toward Vinnie — and the wooden planks beneath me rocked and rolled, tossing me like a beach ball on an ocean wave.

"I'm not going to give up!" I dragged myself across the floor on my belly. Inched my way toward Vinnie — and felt the floor heave up. It hurled me across the room. Slammed me hard into the wall.

"Brandon — watch out!"

I rolled away from the wall — as it moved in on me.

I froze, terrified, as all the walls moved. Creaking loudly. Moving fast now. Moving in to crush us to death.

"Vinnie, get out of that chair!" I cried. "We have to get out of here!"

"I can't," he wailed.

I reached out to the arm of a couch. Used it to pull myself up. Held on to the couch as support to make my way to Vinnie.

The floor pitched violently. The couch bounced up and down as I clung to it.

I inched my way forward.

The walls closed in. The room was getting smaller. Smaller.

If I stretch out my arms, I could touch a wall with each hand, I realized with horror.

I glanced at Vinnie. He cowered in the chair. Frozen with fear.

I was almost there. Almost to Vinnie. Just a few feet away.

"Give me your hand, Vinnie!" I shouted as the floor hurled me backwards.

Vinnie shook his head no.

"Please, Vinnie! Do it! Give me your —"

"Oh, noooo!" Vinnie gazed up at the ceiling and moaned.

I stared up at it too — and saw it rumbling down toward me.

The floor quaked wildly — and sent me crashing to my knees. I fell hard — on top of the flashlight. As the floor rocked, the flashlight rolled away.

I stabbed my hand out, desperate for something to hold on to. And I grabbed the flashlight.

Another frantic thought crashed into my terrified mind.

How will the ghost react to light?

Ghosts live in darkness, don't they? I asked myself.

This house is so dark.

If I shined the light . . .

Could I force the ghost to retreat? Could I distract it long enough to let Vinnie and me escape?

Light. Yes . . . light.

The floor bounced me against the wall. The ceiling was inches away from my head now.

In front of me, Vinnie's chair spun, whirling faster and faster. Vinnie gripped the chair arms, and spun so fast, he became a blur.

"Help . . . ," he murmured weakly. "Oh, help . . ."

"No!" I gasped as the flashlight bounced out of my hand.

I dropped to the pulsing, curling floor — and grabbed it again.

It's worth a try, I told myself. It's our only hope.

I slid my hand up the side of the flashlight — and clicked it on.

And cried out in horror when nothing happened.

The batteries were dead.

"No! No! No!" I screamed, so frustrated and angry.

I slammed the flashlight against the floor.

And the light flashed on.

It flickered, weak at first. I shook the flashlight hard, and the light brightened.

Struggling to stand on the throbbing, tossing floor, I raised the flashlight and swept the beam of light over the wall.

Would it work?

28

To my surprise, the wall pulled back.

I moved the light beam to the floor. I uttered a happy cry as the floor stopped moving and flattened out.

"Yes! Yes!" I shrieked.

I turned and beamed the light at Vinnie's chair — and the chair began to shrink.

Vinnie jumped up. "It let go of me!" he cried.

The chair shrank lower, lower — and vanished into the floor.

"Let's go!" I cried.

I grabbed Vinnie's hand and ran, pulling him to the door.

The walls began sliding in on us again. But I swung the beam of light from wall to wall, and they dropped back into place.

We ran through the door. And down the long hall.

And seconds later, we were back outside, back in the cool, fresh air. Running, running hard, away from the haunted house, down the street still filled with shouting, laughing trick-or-treaters.

I've saved two frightened people, I realized.

I have only one more to go. But I know there can't be much time left. Maybe only minutes . . . or seconds!

Vinnie and I ran until we reached his house. He thanked me for saving him. Thanked me again and again.

But I hardly listened. My brain was whirring.

How can I save someone else? What can I do?

I watched Vinnie go running into his house. Would his parents believe his wild story? Probably not. But I didn't have time to worry about that.

I needed to rescue one more person. If only I knew how much time was left . . .

"Leave me alone!"

"Huh?" I turned and saw a group of costumed kids across the street.

"Leave me alone!" my sister Maya screamed again.

Some big, tough-looking kids had Maya and her friends surrounded. I saw one of them push Maya's friend and grab her trick-or-treat bag.

Another big guy grabbed my sister's arm and twisted it behind her back.

Maya let out a frightened cry.

I'll scare these guys away, I decided, and I'll have my three rescues. I'll be okay. I'll be alive!

I slid my head under my coat. The old headless gag should do it, I told myself.

I zipped the coat over my head. Then I tore

across the street, screaming, "My head! My head!"

I heard laughter.

"Brandon — stop joking! Help us!" Maya wailed.

I poked my head up. The tough kids were laughing at my headless trick. They weren't scared at all.

Now what? I asked myself.

One of them — a big, powerful-looking kid with red hair standing straight up on his head like a broom — grabbed the front of my coat. "What do you want to do with him, Chris?" he asked one of his pals.

"I like him better *without* a head," a blond boy, wearing blue sunglasses despite the darkness, replied with a sneer.

"Let's take off his head," the red-haired guy said, tightening his grip on me.

"L-let me go," I stammered. "And leave the girls alone too. Pick on someone your own —"

"Shut up, geek!" the red-haired boy bellowed.

"Make him climb that tree," another boy suggested.

They grabbed me and shoved me roughly against the tree trunk.

"No — please," I begged. "I don't have time. You have to let me go. I —"

If they force me up the tree, I won't stand a chance, I realized. I won't be able to rescue anyone. And I'll go back to the other side . . . forever.

"Get up there," the boy named Chris barked. "Start climbing."

"No —" I tried to squirm away.

But they were too strong. The red-haired boy pushed me back against the tree. "Climb! Fast!"

I'm doomed, I realized.

I'm dead.

And then — something *really* horrible happened.

"Get up that tree. All the way to the top!" The red-haired boy gave me another shove from behind.

I felt his hand push my shoulder — and then . . . and then . . .

I felt my shoulder slide off.

The shoulder slid forward and then started to fall.

I uttered a startled gasp as my head slid off. My shoulders . . . my chest . . .

I stood and stared, so confused. I watched my body crumple to the grass. It sprawled onto its side and didn't move.

I stood there in amazement — staring down at my body.

Staring until I finally realized what had happened.

Time was up!

The hour had ended. I failed. Failed! Once again, I'd slipped from my body.

And now I stood gazing down at myself in horror.

A scream made me look up.

The tough guys were staring at me with bulging eyes. They gaped down at my fallen body — and then up at me.

And then they tossed back their heads in horrified screams.

They all were screaming now — the tough guys, Maya, and Maya's three friends.

Then they all spun away from the terrifying sight, staggering and stumbling, desperate to get away.

I watched them run screaming down the street. The boys went one way. Maya and her friends headed for our house.

"I did it!" I cried out loud. "I saved three people! I rescued three frightened people! I did it! I did it!" I knew that the hour had already ended, but I hoped Norb would give me a break.

I hid my body under a bush. "I'll be back for you in a minute!" I told it happily.

Then I took off, running to the ravine. "I did it!" I announced at the top of my lungs as I made my way past Mr. Benson's house. "I did it! I saved three people!"

I stopped at the edge and peered across. "Hey,

Norb!" I shouted. "Norb — where are you? I did it! I'm back!"

Out of the darkness, Norb appeared on the other side. He still wore the ugly monster mask. He waved to me. "Jump across, Brandon," he called. "Hurry. You can do it. Jump across."

"Okay," I agreed. I stepped back and took a running start. At the edge of the ravine, I leaped — and made it easily to the other side.

"Welcome back," Norb said, his eyes studying me from inside the mask.

"I did it!" I exclaimed. "I saved three frightened people. Now get me back inside my body!"

Norb laughed. "Oops — just joking!" he declared.

I gaped at him. "Huh? What did you say?"

"Oops — just joking!" he repeated. He laughed harder.

The other masked kids suddenly appeared behind him. They were laughing too.

"But you said —" I pleaded.

"Oops — just joking!" Norb cried gleefully.

I swallowed hard. I was trembling so hard, I could barely speak. "You mean —?" I choked out.

"Don't you get it, Brandon?" Norb asked. He reached both hands up — and tugged off his mask.

"Nooooo!" I let out a scream as his face came into view.

My face!

I stared at *my* face!

112

Norb tossed back his head and laughed. "Happy Halloween!" he shouted. "Happy Halloween, Brandon!"

And then he reached both hands up and pulled off the face.

It was a mask! Only a rubber mask!

And underneath . . . nothing but air. He was headless!

"This year, I dressed up as *you*," Norb said. His voice seemed to come out of nowhere. "Didn't you guess? Didn't you figure it out when I told you my name — Norband? It's Brandon. I just moved the letters around!"

I opened my mouth, but no sound came out.

The other kids all laughed. And then they too pulled off their masks.

I groaned. Their faces were all decayed, crumbling. Rotting away. Patches of green skin clinging to yellowed bone. Empty eye sockets. Slack jaws with missing teeth . . .

"You're all dead," I choked out.

"And so are you," Norb said softly. "You're one of us now, Brandon. You're one of us *forever*."

I stared at him, letting it all sink in.

They played a joke on me, a Halloween joke.

There was never a chance I'd get my body back.

A long sigh escaped my throat. I narrowed my eyes at Norb. "Well . . . it's still Halloween, right?" I asked.

"Yes," he replied.

"And we're all dead, right?" I asked.

"Yes," he replied again.

"So, come on!" I cried, slapping him on the back. "Let's cross over to the other side and do some *serious* scaring!"

About R.L. Stine

R.L. Stine is the most popular author in America. He is the creator of the *Goosebumps, Give Yourself Goosebumps, Fear Street,* and *Ghosts of Fear Street* series, among other popular books. He has written nearly 200 scary novels for kids. Bob lives in New York City with his wife, Jane, teenage son, Matt, and dog, Nadine.

Welcome to the new millennium of fear

Goosebumps®
SERIES 2000

Check out this
chilling preview of
what's next from
R.L. STINE

Attack of the
Graveyard Ghouls

5

here is my backpack?" I heard Jason's shrill voice from down the hall.

I was sitting in front of my computer after dinner, finishing an English paper. Downstairs, I could hear my little brother and sister crying. And I could hear Mom sounding very stern: "I won't talk to you two till you stop crying. Now, stop it! Please!"

I tried to shut out all the noise and concentrate on my homework. But Jason popped his head into my room. "Where is my backpack?" he demanded.

"How should I know?" I lied.

"I need it for tomorrow, and it isn't in my closet," Jason whined.

I stared hard at him. Thinking. Thinking . . .

And I realized where his backpack was. I'd left it up in the graveyard!

"It was right on my shelf!" Jason cried. "And I need it tomorrow morning." His voice was climbing higher and higher.

"Uh . . . I think I know where it is," I confessed.

I shut my eyes. I pictured myself in the graveyard this morning. I set the stupid backpack down against a tree.

When I thought that a hand grabbed my ankle, my baseball cap flew off, I remembered. But I didn't stop to pick it up. I ran out of there as fast as I could. And I forgot all about the backpack too.

Now what?

"Go get it!" Jason demanded angrily. He tried to pull me up by the shoulders. "You're not allowed to borrow my stuff. Go get it, Spencer — or I'm telling!"

I could still hear Remy and Charlotte crying downstairs and Mom screaming at them to stop.

If I tell Mom I took Jason's backpack and left it in the graveyard, she'll *kill* me! I decided.

"No problem," I told my brother. "Calm down. I'll go get it."

Why did I say that? Was I really going to climb up to the Highgrave cemetery at night?

Did I have a choice?

I sent Jason back to his room so I could think. Then I paced back and forth in my little room, three steps one way, three steps back, my mind racing.

I can't go up there alone, I knew.

Once again, I felt the cold fingers tightening around my ankle.

No. No way I can go to the graveyard alone.

I took a deep breath, picked up the phone, and punched Audra's number. "Could you do me a little favor?" I blurted as soon as she picked up.

"A favor? Who is this? Spencer?"

"Yeah. It's me. Can you come up to the graveyard with me — for just a second? I need to get a couple of things up there."

There was a very long pause on her end. Then, finally, Audra said, "You're joking — right?"

I told Mom and Dad I was going over to Audra's to do homework. Then I slipped out the backdoor, zipping my jacket against the cold wind that blew down from the hillside.

I tested my flashlight as I trotted through the backyards. It sent an orange circle of light over the frosty grass.

Audra met me at the side of her garage. She wore a heavy down parka, and she had her hair tucked under a wool ski cap.

"Are we really going up to the graveyard to get a baseball cap and a backpack?" she asked, shaking her head.

"I already explained," I said, shining the flashlight in her face. "It's the backpack I *have* to get. I never should have borrowed the stupid thing from Jason in the first place."

We leaned into the wind and began our climb. The tall grass up the hillside was slick from the frosty dew. Audra grabbed my arm and we made our way up slowly.

"Frank called me right after you did," she said.

"Huh? What did *he* want?" I asked.

"He wanted to borrow my history notes. But I told him I was going up to the graveyard with you." Audra laughed. "Frank sounded really surprised."

"Why did you tell him what we were doing?" I demanded.

She shrugged but didn't answer. We stepped around a clump of scraggly, bare trees. Their limbs trembled in the wind, making a soft creaking sound.

"Why did you scream up in the graveyard this morning?" Audra asked. "Tell me the truth this time."

"Huh, me? Scream? I . . . uh . . . thought I saw something."

"You don't believe in those graveyard ghouls you wrote about in your English paper, do you?" Audra's green eyes studied me.

"No way," I muttered.

I gazed up to the top of Highgrave Hill. No

strange flickering lights tonight. No eerie mist. The moon floated low in a clear black sky.

We stopped as we walked through the open gate.

I swept my flashlight over a row of old tombstones. They tilted against each other as if asleep.

I jumped as something leaped out from the bottom of a tall, narrow gravestone.

A rabbit.

Audra laughed. "Spencer — you jumped a mile! It's only a little bunny rabbit."

"Let's grab the backpack and get out of here," I murmured. "I'm pretty sure I left it near that double grave."

A cloud rolled over the moon. I struggled to see as the graveyard darkened. I raised the beam of light and swept it along the rows of graves.

"I wish I brought a flashlight too," Audra whispered. I saw her shiver. "It's so dark up here now."

"Just stick close to me," I said. I felt as frightened as Audra did, but I'd never let her know that.

The wind whistled as it blew through the gnarled, old graveyard trees. The bare limbs shook and creaked. Tall grass brushed against the tilting gravestones, making a *SHUSSSSH SHUSSSSH* sound.

We made our way along a row of low graves. "Oh!" I cried out as my left foot sank into a hole. Pain shot up from my ankle. I rubbed the foot till it stopped hurting.

"I'm okay. Just twisted it a little," I explained.

I climbed a low rise and turned into the next row. And spotted the backpack on the ground, resting against a bent, old tree.

I hurried over to it, kneeled down, and grabbed it up with both hands. The dew had frozen on it, spreading a thin layer of frost over the canvas. I brushed it off with one hand.

I could hear Audra breathing hard behind me — loud, rasping breaths.

"What's wrong?" I asked. "Why are you out of breath?"

She didn't reply.

I continued brushing the frost off the backpack. But I stopped when I heard leaves rustling in front of me.

I raised my eyes to the sound. I gazed down the row of tombstones — as someone stepped out quickly from behind a tree.

"Who —?" I uttered.

Too dark to see.

The figure moved toward me, taking long strides.

"Audra!" I cried, finally recognizing her. "What were you doing over there?"

But then a more frightening question burst into my mind: If Audra was over by the tree, *who was breathing so hard behind me?*

With a cry, I spun around.

No one there. No one.

Someone stood breathing hard behind me, I knew. Loud, raspy breaths. So close behind.

If it wasn't Audra, who was it? Where did they go?

A chill ran down my back. The backpack slid out of my hand. I bent to pick it up.

When I stood, Audra had vanished again.

"Audra? What's going on?" I cried.

"Sorry." Her voice rose up from a grassy slope. "I lost you in the dark, Spencer. There is a really awesome gravestone here. You should check it out."

I swung the backpack onto my shoulders. Then I raised the flashlight and aimed it in Audra's direction.

She was bent over a tiny gravestone carved in black. "It's a little baby grave," she called, her voice muffled in the rush of wind. "And it has a long lullabye engraved on the stone. It . . . it's so sad, Spencer."

"That baby probably died a hundred years ago," I muttered. I started over to her, the circle of orange light from the flashlight bouncing off the gravestones. "I found the stupid backpack. We can go, Audra."

"Okay. Just come take a look at this," she called.

Fiddling with the backpack, I started along the row of graves toward her. But the light beam stopped on something on the ground.

My cap! My baseball cap.

I had forgotten all about it.

"All right!" I cried happily.

I bent down. Scooped it off the grass.

And screamed.

Resting snugly inside the cap — a head!

A real human head!

7

ark, sunken eyes stared at me. The mouth hung open loosely, revealing black toothless gums.

My stomach heaved. I started to gag.

My hands began to shake, and the head dropped out of the cap. It bounced against my shoe and rolled into the grass.

"A . . . head!" I choked out. Too weak for Audra to hear.

"Spencer, what are you doing?" she called through the darkness.

My stomach heaved again. I could still see those blank, sunken eyes.

"Audra . . . help!" I gasped. "A head. Someone's head in my cap!"

"Huh?" I heard the crunch of leaves. Audra came running over. "I can't hear you, Spencer."

"Look —" I waved the cap in my hand.

"Is that your cap?" she asked, narrowing her eyes at me.

"The head...," I murmured through chattering teeth. "A real head!" I pointed.

She gazed down at the grass. "Where?"

The flashlight trembled in my hand. I struggled to hold the light steady. "There!" I cried.

Holding the sides of her ski cap, Audra squinted into the light. Then she turned back to me. "I don't see anything, Spencer."

I stared down, moving the light in slow circles over the grass. No...no...no...

No head.

Vanished.

But I knew I had seen it. Those cold, sunken eyes stayed in my mind.

"Graveyard ghouls," I murmured. "I...I thought it was some kind of legend. You know, a creepy ghost story everyone in town shared. But —"

Audra placed a hand on the shoulder of my coat. "Spencer, take it easy. You're shaking all over."

I opened my mouth to reply — but a sound made me stop.

A scraping, scratching sound, followed by soft thuds.

And then, a voice moaned on the wind, "Spencer...give...me...back...my...head!"

8

"**N**oooo!"

I screamed. Spun around.

I heard high-pitched laughter. And saw Frank Foreman step into the row of graves. Buddy Tanner followed close behind him, along with two big, beefy guys I recognized from school.

"Well? Give me back my head!" Frank declared. They burst out laughing all over again.

"How long were you standing there?" I choked out. "What are you *doing* here?"

Frank grinned at Audra. "Audra told me you two were coming up here for a picnic. So how come we weren't invited?"

"It's not a picnic," Audra snapped. "I told you not to come, Frank."

"We're leaving now, anyway," I said. I started toward the gate.

Frank moved quickly to block my path. "You sure, Spencer?" he taunted. "You sure you're leaving?"

"Give us a break, guys," Audra pleaded. "You're not funny. It's cold up here and —"

"And there really are ghouls," I blurted out.

I was sorry the moment I said it.

Why did I let that slip? I knew they'd never let me forget it for the rest of my life!

"Ghouls?" Buddy sneered. "Hey, Frank, he really believes that stuff."

"Of course he does," Frank replied, grinning at me. "That's because Spencer *is* a ghoul!"

"Let us go!" I insisted.

But Frank grabbed me by the shoulders. The flashlight fell from my hand. It clattered against a tombstone, hit the ground, and went out.

"Spencer doesn't want to leave," Frank insisted.

"Because he's a ghoul," Buddy added. "He's a graveyard ghoul."

"Spencer is a ghoul," the other two guys repeated.

"Get lost!" I yelled, hoping I sounded brave. I jerked free of Frank's grasp. I grabbed Audra's hand, ready to run.

"Come on, Spencer. You know you don't want to leave," Frank insisted. "You want to stay here, right? With the other ghouls?"

"Leave him alone," Audra demanded.

"Hey — we're just kidding around here," Frank told her. He grabbed me and pinned me against a tree.

"What's the big idea?" I cried, starting to sweat despite the cold.

Then I saw that one of the other guys had a rope — and my legs began to shake.

"What are you going to do?" Audra screamed. "Leave him alone. This isn't funny! Come on, Spencer. Let's get out of here."

Frank pulled me away from the tree and shoved me up against a tall gravestone. I could feel the cold stone through my jacket.

I swung my arm to hit Frank.

But Buddy and another boy grabbed me. They pinned my arms behind me.

I kicked my legs. I tried to yank free, but Frank's friends held on tightly.

"You're going too far!" Audra shrieked. "This isn't a joke, Frank! You can't do this to him!"

Frank laughed.

Audra turned to me. "Don't worry, Spencer. I'm going for help." She spun away from us and vanished through the cemetery gate.

"Let me go!" I yelled, twisting and turning, fighting to free myself.

"Graveyard ghoul. Graveyard ghoul." The boys chanted as they wound the rope around me, tying me tightly to the gravestone.

"Let me go." I kicked out as hard as I

could. But that made them pull the rope even tighter.

"Bye, ghooooul!" Frank howled. Then they all raced out of the graveyard and down Highgrave Hill.

This can't be happening! I thought, struggling to free myself.

Tied to a gravestone in Highgrave Cemetery in the middle of the night!

"Wait! Please!" I called to them.

"Don't leave me up here!" My heart pounded in my chest. I felt the gravestone on my back, so cold, so cold . . .

"Please — come back!"

9

"Frank, come back! Hey — guys!" I screamed.

I could hear them laughing as they ran down the hill.

"Help me! Hey — guys! Don't leave me here!" I pleaded.

I tugged at the ropes, screaming for help.

A fluttering sound above my head made me freeze.

I felt a rush of cold air against my face. Another flutter, and something flickered against my cheek.

Bats!

Dozens of chittering bats. My shouts had scared them — and sent them flying from the trees.

I tried to duck as they darted low over my head. I saw flaring red eyes — and felt another rush of cold wind against my face.

Back and forth they swooped, chittering, whistling, their wings fluttering so close.

"Please —" I choked out. "Please —"

Another low swoop. Another flash of tiny red eyes.

And then they vanished into the treetops.

Silence now.

Except for the rapid thudding of my heart.

"Spencer, stay calm," I said out loud. "You're not going to be out here all night. Someone will rescue you. Audra went to get help. She will bring someone. They will be up here really soon."

The bitter wind of Highgrave Hill picked up. It whipped the dead, brittle leaves on the ground. It blew dirt up into my face.

The old trees creaked and groaned.

A long, low moan from nearby made my heart skip a beat.

"Where is Audra?" I asked out loud. "What's taking her so long?"

I peered out over the dark tombstones, searching frantically for her.

Where *is* she? Did she decide to leave me out here? She wouldn't do that.

Would she?

I pushed forward, trying to loosen the rope. It was wound around me tightly, from my shoulders to just below my knees. It pressed my hands tight against my sides.

I heaved my chest forward as hard as I could. But the rope wouldn't give at all.

I twisted and turned my shoulders, trying to loosen it. But it remained taut.

With all my strength, I pushed my hands out. But the rope cut through the skin on my knuckles.

"What's the use?" I fell back against the cold gravestone with a bitter sigh.

I stared out at the old tombstones bathed in the light of the full moon.

"Huh?"

Did a gravestone just shift? Did it tilt to one side?

"No. It looked as if it moved. But it didn't," I re-assured myself. "It's just an illusion, caused by the shimmering light of the moon."

But I blinked hard and stared at it — just to make sure. The tombstone beside it appeared to tilt now!

I heard another long moan, closer this time.

The trees creaked. The wind shook their scrag-gly, bare limbs.

Another tombstone shifted. With a low creak, it seemed to lean back.

Another eerie moan, so close . . . so close behind me.

"No!" My head began to pound.

I have to get out of here!

I twisted and turned and pushed against the rope.

"Somebody — help me! Get me *out* of here!"

I gasped as a green mist rose up from the creaking, tilting graves. Slowly at first. Then faster. Thicker. Billowing up with a sour, sick smell.

The stench grew stronger as the mist swirled around me. I started to choke. I cried out as it settled on my face, stinging my skin, burning my eyes.

Break free, Spencer, I ordered myself. No matter what it takes!

But before I could start tugging, a hoarse voice echoed through the sickening mist: *"I . . . need . . . your . . . body."*

PREPARE TO BE SCARED

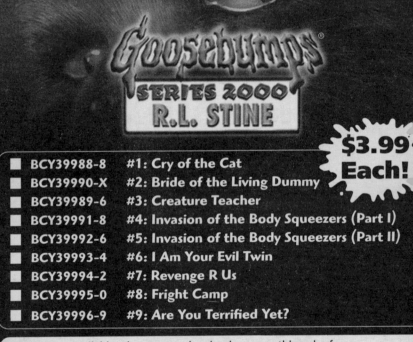

Goosebumps®
SERIES 2000
R.L. STINE

$3.99 Each!